Let Me Love Again

CHOICE BOOKS
The Best In Family Reading
P. O. Box 503
Goshen, IN 46526
We Welcome Your Response

Julia ran and knelt down by Alexandra and the older woman put her arms around her. "Tell me what is troubling you, Julia."

Julia hardly knew where to start. "I'm so confused. I still grieve for Neal, yet I think I am falling in love with Adam. I believe he cares for me..." Alexandra began to say something. "No, please, don't say anything until I tell you everything. Has Adam told you about Georgina?"

Joan Winmill Brown, who first gained recognition as an English actress, has most recently received plaudits for her skill as an editor and compiler of Christian anthologies. Her reading audience will be delighted with her most recent work in the area of Christian romance novels as she writes from her interesting background.

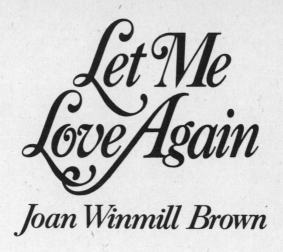

Let Me Love Again

Joan Winmill Brown

HARVEST HOUSE PUBLISHERS
Eugene, Oregon 97402

LET ME LOVE AGAIN

Copyright © 1984 by Joan Winmill Brown
Published by Harvest House Publishers
Eugene, Oregon 97402

ISBN 0-89081-439-2

Printed in the United States of America.

Chapter
—1—

Through the windows of Julia Marshall's tenth-floor apartment, Central Park could be seen donning its winter mantle. New York was experiencing its first major snowfall of the season. Blessedly, the pure white covering hid many of the flaws that the years had ravaged and the scene was one of breathtaking beauty. Towering trees, their branches now beginning to strain beneath the weight of the snow, stood like silent, majestic sentinels in the twilight.

Julia peered down at Fifth Avenue, watching the late Friday afternoon traffic turn the pure white snow into a depressing slush. She turned her eyes back to the virginal beauty of the park. Children were already sledding down one of the steep banks near the round pond. Julia watched as they tirelessly took their sleds to the top and repeatedly skimmed over the freshly fallen snow.

Switzerland, she thought. *It reminds me of Switzerland.* For a moment she was taken back to the country where she and Neal had spent their honeymoon and a sad smile lingered on her lovely young face.

Her mother had insisted on an enormous wedding, and Neal had thought it was an excellent idea—"Anything to be in my future mother-in-law's good graces—plus my own mother's." Mrs. Marshall would feel cheated if her only son and his bride couldn't be shown off to as many guests as possible.

"Besides," Neal had whispered, "I want our families and friends to share in our joy. You'll make the most beautiful bride—ever!"

Finally, Julia could only agree to the idea of such an overwhelming social wedding. She had pictured a very intimate affair, just for the family and a few close friends, but her mother had swept her along with all the planning and details, and Julia had patiently let her enjoy the excitement of it all.

The wedding had been one of the most spectacular of the year, and the *Times* had carried a large photograph of Julia and Neal's radiant faces, followed by a two column article detailing the event.

After the reception, a helicopter had landed among the guests assembled in the garden of Julia's family estate, and had whisked the newly married couple high above a sea of happy faces and taken them, like some "high-tech charger," to J.F.K. Airport and connected them with their flight to Geneva, Switzerland.

Their landing in Geneva had made the feeling of unreality intensify. Driving along the shore of the sparkling blue lake, Julia was captivated with the towering snowcapped mountains and the fairy-tale parks, ablaze with a dazzling display of glorious flowers and shrubs.

Turning to look at Neal as he concentrated on his driving, she had said ecstatically, "Are we really here? Am I really Mrs. Neal Marshall?" Their eyes met and all the love they felt for each other seemed to overflow in an electrifying moment.

"Forever," Neal had whispered. "We'll always be together, darling Julia." He had touched her face lovingly, and she had responded with a kiss on his cheek.

"Forever..."

A taxi horn blared down on the street below, and Julia's thoughts returned to the reality of her life today. She pressed her forehead against the icy cold window and felt once more the gnawing grief that never seemed far away. It had only been ten months ago that Neal had left her. So suddenly. Like a knife cutting away part of her, and leaving a void that could not be filled.

The piercing siren of an ambulance making its way up Fifth Avenue, brought vividly into Julia's mind that day when Neal had suffered a heart attack and was gone from her—without even being able to say "goodbye." A congenital condition that had lain dormant for years had mercilessly taken the loving, understanding man, who she had thought would grow old along with her. They had had so much to look forward to...

"God, please forgive me, but I still feel it was so unfair to take him. He was so young..." Tears filled Julia's expressively beautiful, brown eyes, and coursed down her cheeks.

She had gone through all the stages of grief—shock, disbelief, anger, resignation—but acceptance still escaped her. People told her that it would come in time, that one day she would meet someone else and find love again.

One day...

Julia told them she would never, ever be able to find someone like Neal. Their love had been so all-encompassing, so perfect, the thought of loving someone else seemed unfaithful to Neal's memory.

She wiped her eyes and pushed back her long, jet black hair, and walked away from the window. She glanced around the lofty, elegant living room furnished with heirlooms from each of their families, and auction pieces that she and Neal had found such pleasure in purchasing...

"Julia, drop everything! I've just seen the most fantastic desk at Parke Bernet. The auction begins in half an hour. It would be perfect for the living room...."

Neal had telephoned and insisted she join him. The Louis IVth style desk had gone for "a song," as there had been few buyers at the beginning of the auction, and Neal and Julia had been delighted with their purchase.

"I can work in the living room the evenings that I have to, and you can be near to inspire me," Neal had said excitedly. The advertising world was extremely demanding, and when there was a big campaign he often had to bring work home. The guest bedroom had been turned into his office, but with the purchase of the antique desk he had spent more and more time with Julia in their comfortable, yet graceful, living room. She had delighted in decorating it in soft, muted shades of greens and pinks, that were a perfect setting for their antique pieces.

Julia walked over to the desk and ran her hands over the glowing patina of the wood. She remembered Neal's face—his strong hands as he worked over a project—his voice triumphantly announcing, "I do believe this is going to get their attention! Look at this, Julia!" were all so real to her . . . she felt as if she could reach out and touch him.

The telephone rang and Julia realized she had not turned on any lights. Bending over to switch on the desk lamp, she hesitated to answer the persistent ring. It could be her mother, insisting again that Julia come home for the weekend. Each time she did, there had been young men invited that her parents thought might help take Julia's mind off of her loss. It was all so obvious and, far from being a diversion for her, it made the emptiness of her life even more acute.

The telephone continued to ring, and reluctantly Julia reached to answer.

"Julia! So glad I caught you at home."

It was Patrick Fraser, Neal's partner at the advertising agency. Julia had stayed on at the agency and taken over most of Neal's responsibilities.

When she had first applied at Fraser and Marshall's for the position of executive assistant it had been Neal who interviewed her, and from the moment they met each of them had known that here was the person with whom they would share the rest of their life. Neither of them had been able to remember the conversation afterward. Julia only knew she had the position of executive assistant, and a date for dinner with the most handsome man she had ever met.

"Patrick—how nice of you to call. I'm fine. I just took the afternoon off because all the important things had been taken care of. . . ."

"I'm not calling for an explanation, Julia. I just got back from San Francisco and haven't even seen the office, thank goodness. Marianne has planned a quiet dinner, and we wondered if you would like to join us?"

Julia's first inclination was to say no, even though Patrick and Marianne were such close and understanding friends. She knew she could relax with them. They had loved Neal, and the two men had been more like brothers than business partners. The thought of the frozen dinner which awaited her in her own kitchen, compared to Marianne's incredible cooking, made Julia impulsively accept the invitation.

"Tell your gourmet cook I would love to come. I've missed seeing her."

"Great," Patrick replied. "I'll come to pick you up around 7:30—O.K.?"

"Don't spoil me, Patrick. I'll walk over. I'll be fine."

Admonishing her for being such an independent young woman, Patrick told Julia to be careful, concluding with, "See you in a few minutes."

Julia put down the telephone and sighed with relief. An evening spent with them would be far less of a strain than with the group of people her mother would have waiting for her; and Friday nights were always difficult—the start of the weekend. So often Neal and she had made plans for a "getaway."

Julia walked down the long hall, stopping momentarily to straighten a wayward flower that had decided to stubbornly resist the symmetrical arrangement on the small table near her bedroom door.

Deep in thought, she went over to her

closet and chose a winter white dress, which would make her feel as if she were a snow maiden on this wild, cold night. The wide, black belt made her waist seem even more minute. She sat down on the end of the four-poster bed, while she pulled on the high heeled, black leather boots. Memories came flooding into her mind of the day that she and Neal had bought the old bed.

"Julia, we can refinish it—you'll see," Neal had said enthusiastically, observing her un-convinced expression. They had answered an advertisement and in an out-of-the-way barn on Long Island they had found the bed, in a very sorry state, leaning forlornly among other outcast furniture and bales of hay.

Julia rose to her feet, and put her arms around one of the old carved posts. In spite of the hurt of the memory, she laughed. Piece by piece they had brought the bed through the lobby of the snooty apartment house, and each time they had been caught by the super-intendent with a disdainful, incredulous look on his face.

"Priceless, that's what it is," Neal had called out to him. "Rumor has it President Washing-ton planned the Battle of Valley Forge from this very bed!"

Inside the elevator, as it whirred up to their

floor, they had clung to each other laughing, and Neal had suddenly leaned down and kissed her. They had stayed in each other's arms—unaware that the doors had opened and two elderly ladies were watching them—disapprovingly. Neal and Julia had staggered out past them, triumphantly carrying part of the four-poster bed along the corridor leading to their apartment. They had dissolved into uncontrollable laughter.

"What fun we had . . ." Julia whispered. Then, not giving herself time for the satisfaction of more reminiscing, she gathered up her handbag and walked quickly out of the bedroom to the hall closet, and reached for a striking black, wool cape. Draping a royal blue scarf around her face and neck, she glanced in the full length mirror. She did not notice how her exquisite porcelain complexion contrasted with the brilliance of the scarf, nor how lovely she looked. Julia only saw the haunted expression in her enormous, velvety brown eyes, as she prepared, once more, to face another evening without Neal. At twenty-nine, she felt as if she had already lived her life. Now she was trying to fill the hours—trying to forget the pain and loneliness that dogged her like a faithful, unwanted companion.

The doorman touched his hat as Julia emerged from the elevator. "May I get you a taxi, Mrs. Marshall? It's really snowing hard now."

Julia had planned on walking the three blocks to Patrick and Marianne's, but looking up at the blinding snow swirling past the street lights, she decided to accept the offer of a taxi.

She looked out of the taxi as it made its precarious way through the snow. All she could see was Neal. Neal, walking in the snow—laughing with her as they brought home the groceries—still tying his tie as they raced down Fifth Avenue, late for an important appointment.

Julia sighed. *I have to get away from New York. Even if only for a few months. But where. . .?*

● ● ●

The warmth of the Frasers' apartment was so inviting, and Julia shivered once more as Patrick took her cape.

"It's absolutely freezing out there!" she said, her teeth chattering.

"Come and get warm," Patrick said, kissing her on the cheek and leading her into the living room, where a roaring fire made the serene modern furnishings lose their austere countenance. Julia went over to the fireplace to warm her icy hands.

Marianne called from the kitchen, "Sit down and relax—be with you in a moment," and Julia, after asking if she could help and being assured she could not, sank gratefully into the lean, beige couch—stretching out her long, lithe legs toward the fire.

Patrick brought her a steaming mug of hot apple cider. She sipped the welcome drink; the cinnamon scenting the room with its delicious aroma.

"What a perfect drink for tonight," Julia said, wrapping her hands around the mug. "Thank you."

"You are more than welcome, Julia," Patrick answered, with mock chivalry. Then, looking at her with concern, he added, "Are you taking care of yourself?"

"Of course." She turned her face away from him and gazed into the fire. Sometimes loving concern hurt too much. She knew it would be easy to break down in front of him.

"Julia, I want to talk to you about something. Now I have your word you will be honest with me? If the answer is no, I'll understand."

She nodded her head and continued to

watch the flames consume the giant logs in the fireplace.

"I've decided that the agency in San Francisco needs you for a few weeks—if you are willing to go. Some things require your magic touch out there. The staff doesn't seem to be united, and we've got some excellent accounts that should be getting expert attention."

Julia turned back to look at Patrick. "I can hardly believe it. Coming over in the taxi, I was thinking that I had to get away for a while." Her eyes widened with anticipation, as she thought of the possibility of San Francisco.

"I could stay with a very dear friend of my mother's, Alexandra Panov! She was a ballerina with the American Ballet Company, and I've missed seeing her since she moved there several years ago."

Patrick smiled, seeing the light return to Julia's eyes. "It's all settled then. Whenever you decide to go will be fine with me."

Their conversation was interrupted by Marianne's appearance in the dining room. Julia got up and walked over to give her a hug. "I've missed you. Welcome home."

Marianne put her arms around Julia. "I've missed you, too." Then stepping back, she looked at her and a questioning look came into

Marianne's usually blithe blue eyes. "Have you been eating properly? You look as if you've lost more weight."

"It's this dress. It has a very slimming effect, Mother Bee." Julia laughed it off and watched while Marianne put the finishing touches to a beautifully arranged bowl of flowers that she had placed in the center of the dining room table.

It was then that Julia noticed that it was set for four, and she looked up inquiringly at Patrick and Marianne. The door bell rang, just as she was about to ask who the fourth person was.

Patrick went out into the hall and Marianne said casually, "That must be Adam Kingsley. He's a new client from San Francisco. He flew back with us today." Her straightening of knives and forks, and apparent preoccupation with the table did not fool Julia for a moment.

"Marianne . . ." she began, a feeling of entrapment making her want to escape from the apartment—but she was interrupted by Patrick leading someone into the living room.

"Julia, I want you to meet Adam Kingsley, from San Francisco. Adam . . . Julia Marshall."

Julia was taken off guard for a second, as she looked up at the tall, exceptionally handsome, dark blonde-haired man. His presence seemed to fill the Frasers' living room with an aura of strength and vitality.

She reached to take his outstretched hand. Suddenly, Julia felt, for the first time in months, a vibrant young woman again...

Chapter
—2—

Adam Kingsley's hand in Julia's was firm and strong. They both realized that a few seconds more than the usual handshake had gone by, before they released their hold.

"How good to meet you, Julia. I've been hearing what a tremendous asset you are to the agency." Adam's voice was low and distinctive, and had a warm quality that did not escape Julia.

She smiled and thanked him, thinking how very "San Franciscan" he looked in his dark gray flannel suit, which emphasized his attractive suntan and brilliant blue-gray eyes.

I wonder where he managed to get that tan. I thought they only had rain and fog at this time of the year...

Adam had completely disarmed Julia, and the evening changed pace as soon as he had entered the room. Marianne brought in the hors d'oeuvres and they all sat around the fire, making light conversation about the incredible flight to New York.

"It was definitely the roughest I've ever encountered," Adam was saying, and Julia was trying valiantly to concentrate and appear completely composed. She was aware that Patrick and Marianne were being very low-key, and Julia found herself laughing quite naturally at the light banter that was now in progress.

Adam continued, "I'm still trying to get adjusted to all the changes in temperatures I've encountered, during the last few weeks. The trip to Hawaii found me in weather in the 80s—now here I am in New York, after getting used to the rain once more in San Francisco..."

So you got that fabulous tan in Hawaii, Julia thought, and was completely at a loss when she suddenly heard Adam say to her, "Don't you notice that too, Julia?"

"I'm sorry, I lost track of the conversation. You left me back in Hawaii," Julia apologized, and took refuge in another hors d'oeuvre that Marianne was offering to her.

Adam laughed. "I wish we could all be there tonight. But then perhaps you are one of those people who have to have the four seasons in your life."

"On a night like tonight, I could do without at least one of them." Julia smiled, and finally averted her eyes. He was obviously more than impressed with her, and she hoped that adolescent trait—blushing—would not give away the fact that he had also made a very surprising impression on her.

Julia's moment of embarrassment was interrupted by Marianne's shriek of consternation, as she remembered the quiche in the oven.

Seated opposite Adam at the dining table, Julia suddenly realized that he was sitting in the chair that Neal had so often occupied. The thought brought her back to the reality of her life. For about twenty minutes she had been behaving as if she were not a widow, but a carefree young woman—able to enjoy the company of another man and to laugh and relax in the home of friends.

The memory of Neal looking at her across the table and winking in that intimate way

of his when they shared a private moment in
company, made Julia look down at her plate.
She felt she was betraying the love that they
had shared.

Patrick reached out for Julia's hand, as they
said grace. She looked quickly at him, then
Marianne, and took their hands. In their eyes,
she could read volumes of understanding.
Bowing her head, she silently asked the Lord
to calm her, and give her the strength to get
through the evening. Only a slight shaking
of her hand, as she reached for her water glass
revealed the quiet battle going on inside her.

Julia looked over at Marianne, thinking how
radiantly happy she always seemed. In the
glow of the candlelight, her blue eyes were
reminiscent of the sky on a perfect summer
day.

Patrick adored her, and they were the
perfect foil for each other's personality—his
so quiet and rugged, yet determinedly force-
ful when it came to any business transac-
tions—hers so sunny and resolute, always seeing the good in anyone.

Marianne had finally been able to get Julia
interested in the hospital visitation program
at their church. At first Julia had resisted—
not wanting to go near any hospital—afraid
it would be a reminder of Neal's death. But

she had begun by visiting a young woman, who had suffered the loss of not only her husband, but a child too. This had helped Julia take her mind off her own tragedy, and as she read passages of hope and comfort from the Bible to the young woman, Julia found that they had ministered to her need, too.

Fear not, for I am with you...

Now seated opposite Adam, those words came back to quiet her. Julia soon found herself able to enter the conversation, and Adam listened intently to everything she had to say. She noticed behind his laughter there was a look of hurt, that sometimes was unsuccessfully hidden.

Patrick and Adam were discussing politics and what it would be like to run a highly emotional, exhausting campaign—one in which you believed in *everything* you were promising and had mortgaged *everything* you owned, assured that the public was for you—only to be shatteringly defeated at the polls.

"Imagine awakening the next morning..." Patrick said gloomily. "It would definitely be a day that you would want to crawl back into bed, and pull the sheets over your head."

Adam said quietly, "Any kind of rejection is hard to take. As you grow older you learn to smile on the outside, but the hurt is still there. I'm thankful for a faith that tells me I am loved—no matter what happens."

As if he had revealed too much, Adam turned to smile at Marianne. "This quiche is one of the finest I've ever eaten. Patrick is a very fortunate man, in more ways than one, having you."

Marianne thanked him and insisted he take a second slice. She looked over at Julia, and noticed she had hardly eaten any of hers.

"Julia, you don't seem to have the same opinion about my cooking."

"You know better than that. I'm just not very hungry this evening." Julia knew she had been toying with her food. Nothing tasted appetizing to her any more. She smiled at Marianne. "I consider you to be the finest cook I know. One day I'm going to have to take lessons from you."

Julia continued to wonder what lay behind the hurt look that she had seen in Adam's eyes, as he had talked about rejection. *It must have been something quite traumatic. . . and recent.*

Later, dessert was served around the fire. A delicious concoction that Marianne had found in a European cookbook, called "Pears Sabayon." The fruit was encased in a light, fluffy pastry that melted in the mouth, and the golden syrup—topped off with whipped cream—made the dish an epicurean delight. Even Julia found her appetite returning.

"I'll never understand how you can spend the day in a plane, and then casually present a gourmet dinner like this." Julia looked in amazement at Marianne.

"Do you really want to know how I do it?" Julia nodded. "Have plenty of ready-to-go ingredients in your freezer and closets. Serve with 'panache,' and don't tell anyone your secret!"

Adam was sitting next to Julia on the couch, and when he passed her the cream for her coffee their hands touched, sending an exciting tremor racing through her. Disconcerted, she thanked him, and hastily asked him more about his work. She had learned through their conversation at dinner that he was the owner of a fast-growing computer company, based in the Silicon Valley, near San Francisco. He was eager to expand, and felt the necessity for a major advertising campaign.

"Do you want to present a dignified image, or one that will appeal to the vast majority of the computer-seeking public?" Julia asked, aware that her usual businesslike composure and concentration were being sabotaged by the nearness of this vitally attractive man.

"As the machine is designed to appeal to the customer who is desirous of owning a computer, yet does not wish to spend months learning how to master it, I think the latter."

"The latter?" Julia could not remember what she had asked him, and it was obvious. They both laughed. She found herself apologizing once more for her lack of concentration.

"Friday night is hardly the time to be bogged down with business. Let's call a truce until Monday morning on anything that resembles work." Adam smiled at her, a hopeful expression in his eyes. "It's been a few years since I spent any length of time in New York. I was wondering if we could all take in some of the sights tomorrow."

He looked over at Patrick and Marianne, seated opposite, but they both started to speak at once. Tomorrow would be a hectic day for them, as they were due in Connecticut at Marianne's parents for a family get-together. Sunday, however, they would be free after church to escort him wherever he desired.

"Dare I presume on your time?" Adam searched Julia's eyes, that wore a hesitant expression. "I don't want to be a burden..."

"Of course you wouldn't be a burden. I'd be delighted to show you New York. That's if we're not snowed in by tomorrow."

Even as Julia agreed to seeing him, she had mixed emotions. But Saturday spent alone would be harder for her. She found herself looking forward to being with Adam—after all he was to be in New York for only a few days.

Then the realization hit her—she would be going to San Francisco soon, and more than likely be working on his account. The thought of leaving New York now panicked her, and she wondered if she should tell Patrick she had second thoughts about going. Julia looked over at him, watching intently as he put another log on the fire.

I can't let him down. I'll go. I'll call Alexandra Panov tomorrow and ask if I can stay, Julia thought. Alexandra had always been so ready to listen to Julia. She remembered sitting by the fire at the Panov home in Bronxville, New York, sipping tea and dreaming aloud about her future in the world. Studying then at Sarah Lawrence College, Julia had been determined to make her mark in advertising. Alexandra had encouraged her—telling her she could achieve anything she wanted in life, if she were prepared not to be daunted when plans did not always turn out quite as expected.

"Remember, Julia, God has a definite plan for each of our lives. Don't try to shut Him out. . . ."

All Julia's aspirations had been shattered by Neal's death, and she was conscious of the great void in her life—one not only caused by Neal's absence, but a spiritual yearning that never seemed to be fulfilled.

"I've always wanted to skate at Rockefeller Plaza," she heard Adam saying to her.

Quickly, Julia said assuringly, "Your wish can easily be granted. Why don't we go there tomorrow before lunch and work up an appetite?"

"I'd really like that." Adam's eyes seemed to be searching hers, as if questioning whether she was just being polite, or whether she too would find skating enjoyable. "If tomorrow you change your mind, I'll understand."

"Never," she said lightheartedly. "It's one of my favorite things to do in New York in the winter, Neal and I always. . ." Julia looked away, unsure of how she could finish the sentence.

Adam came to the rescue. "I always had favorite places that my ex-fiance and I used to go." He looked at her compassionately, and it was then she knew the reason for the hurt in his vulnerable, searching eyes.

Julia was grateful for his sensitivity. Knowing that he, too, had suffered a loss made it easier for her to relate to him. There

was now a common bond upon which to build
their friendship.

*I don't know how to react to someone, Lord,
who has never known what it is to lose the
dearest person in the world. . .*

Julia noticed it was well after midnight. The
hours had slipped away, and she was thankful
that Patrick and Marianne had invited her.
This Friday night had not been nearly as painful as others.

"I really should be going. It's all right for you
people who are still on Pacific time." She got
to her feet, and immediately Adam jumped up
too.

"May I see you home?"

There was a slight hesitation on Julia's part,
then she said brightly, "Why not? That's kind
of you. Thank you."

She noticed that Patrick and Marianne exchanged glances and there was a mutual smile
between them.

The snow had stopped, and Adam took
Julia's arm to help her across the still-
treacherous streets. A small gale met them as
they turned up Fifth Avenue, and Julia found
herself flung against Adam.

Flustered, she looked up at him and said
breathlessly, "I'm so sorry. . ."

"Please don't be," he said delightedly. "It's

quite the nicest thing that's happened to me in New York."

In spite of her accustomed restraint since Neal's death, Julia found herself laughing. Adam was easy to be with, and she was now looking forward to tomorrow.

They said good night in the lobby of Julia's apartment building. Adam took her hands and said quietly, "I've enjoyed this evening and meeting you."

Julia smiled up at him. "Thank you, Adam." She thought how much she had enjoyed meeting him, too.

"I'll call around 10 o'clock tomorrow morning, and we'll make plans. Until then, sweet dreams, Julia."

He pressed her hands, and once more she felt an exciting tremor race through her. She was conscious of his eyes following her as she walked toward the elevator. Julia felt more alive than she had in months. She waved to him before the door closed.

Julia had noticed that the doorman was smiling, too. It was obvious that he was pleased to see a happy expression on her beautiful young face again. . . .

Chapter
—3—

The gray morning light, filtering through the shades in Julia's bedroom, cast a gloomy atmosphere. But as she awoke, she felt that today would be very special.

She was still hugging Neal's pillow—something she had done ever since he had died. To her it was part of him, and each night she had fallen asleep with her arms wrapped tightly around it.

Julia sat up in bed, pushing back her long, black hair. She stretched her arms above her head and glanced at the clock. It was still only 7 A.M. She had promised herself that she would sleep in, but again there was that excited feeling of anticipation.

She lay back on the pillow and remembered. Adam Kingsley had asked her to go skating. She felt like a teenager again. Part of her wanted to go, but then part of her wished she had never said she would. She had enjoyed meeting him last night. Tracing her fingers along the edge of the pale-blue flowered sheet, she remembered his look of delight when she had been swept against him by the strong gust of wind.

". . . quite the nicest thing that has happened to me in New York!" Julia thought of the laughter they had shared.

She slid out of bed and quickly put on her blue velvet robe, trimmed with white lace. The room was chilly—the heating system, being temperamental, could always be counted on to break down during a cold spell. She walked over to the thermostat and gave it a quick tap—as if that would rectify whatever ailed it. A chuckle escaped her. There would be the long explanations from the janitor and then finally, the heat would be restored. Living in an older, but still exclusive, building had its drawbacks. Neal had always said that you gained, really, as the walls were so much thicker and you didn't have to listen to other people's conversation—or their strange tastes in music.

Julia walked down the corridor to the kitchen, and plugged in the coffee machine. She opened her front door and picked up the *Times* from the doormat. Saturday mornings she always liked to curl up in bed and drink coffee, while reading the newspaper. This morning, however, she found it difficult to concentrate. Questions like, "Where shall we go after we've been to Rockefeller Plaza?"and "What shall I wear?" kept swirling through her head.

Turning to the entertainment section, Julia noticed that Itzhak Perlman was appearing at the Lincoln Center that night. Perhaps Adam might enjoy the Mendelssohn concerto. She knew so little about his personal tastes. Again she thought of Neal, how they instinctively knew what the other one would like.

Julia decided to take a shower. The water beating down on her seemed to help erase memories, but when she got some shampoo in her eyes she was infuriated. Getting out of the shower, she looked quickly in the bathroom mirror. Her eyes looked red-rimmed. She opened the medicine cabinet and reached for the eye drops and hastily applied some—hoping they would work before she met Adam.

Seated at her dressing table, drying her hair, Julia wondered if Adam were awake yet. California time was only 5 A.M. He would probably still be sleeping. She pictured him in bed; his blond, curly hair ruffled from the pillow—looking like a young, innocent little boy.

Embarrassed at her thoughts, she walked to the window and looked down on the ever-changing scene outside. People were already in the park. Some throwing snowballs, others building snowmen. Children were sledding once more. It was another world in New York when the snow came. People flocked to the park to forget their problems, and return to their youth.

The telephone rang and Julia looked over at it, wondering if it could possibly be Adam. It was still only 8:45 A.M.

It was her mother. "Julia, where were you last night? I tried calling you again and again."

"I was over at the Frasers', Mother. They had a client there for dinner and we were discussing some business."

"Well, we really missed you, Julia. There were several people here whom I know you would have loved meeting. Perhaps next weekend . . ."

"Mother, I have to go to San Francisco for a few weeks. The agency needs me there and I've promised Patrick, although it's not definite yet what day I'll be going."

Her mother sighed. "Don't tell me you'll be gone for Thanksgiving, Julia?"

"Possibly. But I'm going to telephone Alexandra today, and see if I can stay with her while I'm in San Francisco."

"That's a wonderul idea, Julia. How she would love to see you. It's been very lonely for her these last few years. I still can't understand why she moved out there, when so many of her friends are here on the East Coast. Now, Julia, can we expect you for dinner tomorrow?" Her voice had taken on an insistent tone.

Julia thought quickly. "I still have this client in town, Mother. Let me call you later. I'll ask if he would like to drive out and see some of Long Island."

"That would be fine, Julia. Is he an older man?"

"I would say around thirty-two or three, Mother."

"How interesting!"

Before her mother could comment further,

Julia responded, "I'll call you later this morning, Mother..."

Julia put down the telephone and smiled. Her mother was such an obvious matchmaker. Very well-meaning, but oh, so obvious. Julia hoped if she took Adam there for dinner he would not be embarrassed by it all. She knew she would be.

Julia continued to brush her hair, then impulsively she plaited it in a long, thick French braid—deciding it would look more casual for her date with Adam. She found a white, knitted hat with an enormous pom-pom and matching scarf. They would help keep the chill winds away, and be perfect with her scarlet tartan jacket and black wool pants. Laying them all on the bed she went to search through the hall closet for her skates. They were under a mountain of boxes, and she had difficulty pulling them out.

With all the usual promises to herself that she would be ruthless and throw out most of the things piled in the closet, she took the skates into the kitchen and found some white shoe polish. Julia had always loved skating, ever since she was a young girl. The whole family had enjoyed it when the small lake on their estate had frozen over. She smiled, thinking of how many times she had fallen trying valiantly to keep up with everyone else.

"It's just like falling off a horse, Julia," her father would say. "You just have to get right up and try again."

Julia had and turned out to be the best skater in the family. The same resilience in her personality had determinedly kept her from being completely shattered by Neal's death. That and her faith. But she knew that in this she was flailing, like a drowning person. There had to be more to Christianity than resignation.

Julia finished polishing the left skate, and was pleased with the results. She thrust her hand deep down into the right one, and felt some paper in it. Puzzled, she drew it out and saw that it was folded and addressed to her in Neal's handwriting.

For a moment, she just stood looking at it in amazement. Tears quickly formed, and she walked over to the kitchen table and sat down. Neal had often written Julia notes—especially if he were going on a trip without her. They would be found in her lingerie drawer, on her pillow—or in her Bible.

Once he had tucked a note in her powder compact, and she had opened it to inconspicuously powder her nose at a stuffy client's meeting. The note, complete with masses of hearts drawn all over it, had fluttered down to rest at the feet of the chairman of the board of one of their top accounts. A man with not one iota of a sense of humor. Julia had had to bite her lip to stop laughing as he ceremoniously handed it back to her.

But this note, so long undiscovered, did not make her smile. Julia felt a great jolt go through her heart as she began to read—

Julia darling:

We've just come back from skating and I wanted to say you were the most beautiful girl there.

Since it's the last day of the season, will you promise me a date at Rockefeller Plaza the minute it opens again?

I'll have that to look forward to...

Julia could no longer see through her tears to read on. Burying her head in her arms on the table, she cried inconsolably. For Neal, that opening day never came.

"Oh, Neal, why did you have to leave me?"

It seemed each time she was beginning to get over her loss, something unexpected like this would happen, and she would be right back at the agonizing realization once more.

The telephone rang—precisely at 10 A.M. Julia knew it was Adam. How could she go skating with him now? Neal's note had taken away any joy of being with Adam—especially at Rockefeller Plaza.

Trying to control her voice, she answered softly, "Hello?"

"Julia, what's wrong?"

There were a few moments of silence and then, through her tears, Julia whispered, "I can't go skating with you. I hope you'll understand..."

"Of course, Julia. Is there anything I can do to help?"

The tenderness in his voice caused Julia to break down again.

"Let me come over and talk about whatever has upset you so much."

Julia found herself agreeing. "Thank you, Adam. Something happened this morning that brought back a great deal of heartache. Please forgive me."

"There's nothing to forgive. I'll be right over."

He was staying at the St. Moritz Hotel, so Julia knew she would not have long before he arrived. She went to the refrigerator for some ice cubes. Wrapping them in a tea towel she placed them over her eyes, hoping the swelling would go down. She had been foolish to agree to Adam's coming over. She should have waited until she had complete control before seeing him.

Realizing she was still not dressed, Julia hurried into the bedroom and proceeded to put on the clothes she had selected earlier. Now they seemed all so wrong, but she did not care. Nothing mattered. Neal's note had devastated her.

In what seemed only a few minutes, her doorbell rang. Reluctantly, she went to answer it.

Adam stood there, his eyes filled with concern and understanding.

Julia looked up at him, her eyes bright with tears. The sight of her looking so utterly desolate made Adam reach out to her with both hands. She went to him, and the enormity of her sorrow made the tears flow unchecked. The warmth of his arms around her filled Julia with a feeling of comfort she had missed—for so many months.

Chapter
—4—

The note from Neal was still laying on the kitchen table, and Julia walked deliberately over to it and picked it up. Without looking at Adam, she said softly, "I found this note from my husband, tucked into one of my ice skates. He put it there just after we had skated together..." Then almost inaudibly, "...for the last time."

Adam stood leaning against the kitchen doorway, watching Julia intently. "Of course I understand why you wouldn't want to go skating today, Julia. It must have been a tremendous shock for you."

"It was. He was always leaving me notes, but this one—well, I felt for a split second that he was still alive." She looked up at Adam. "I'm so sorry to burden you with all this. It's hardly the right way to start a business relationship with someone."

Adam walked over to Julia and said gently, "I hope you will regard me as a friend. One who knows, too, a little of what it is to have your dreams turned to ashes overnight." His jaw tightened momentarily, and he looked away from Julia—as if not wanting her to see the pain he still felt.

"Last night during dinner, you said you knew you were loved—even though you had faced rejection." Adam nodded. "If it's not too painful to talk about it, what exactly did you mean?"

Adam drew in a deep breath, and Julia went to apologize, but he put his hand on her shoulder. "I'm glad you've asked, because it gives me an opportunity to tell you about something that has happened in my life—quite recently."

He went over and sat down at the table facing Julia. "I mentioned my ex-fiancee to you last night. Well, we had been engaged for over a year, when she had to go to Europe on business. All the plans for the wedding were in progress. Georgina . . ." He found it difficult to mention her name, and paused long enough to clear his throat. "Well, she either called me each night, or I called her. Then for three days I lost contact with her. I was very worried, and called several friends in France to locate her. Eventually, one of them called me to say she had been seen in the company of a Frenchman—an extremely handsome man, with quite a reputation."

Adam's face had become tense, as he remembered hearing the news. "Finally, after about a week, Georgina called me and told me she had met someone else, and that the wedding was off."

Instinctively, Julia put her hand on his. "I'm sorry, Adam."

"Thank you." He smiled that sad smile that she had seen at dinner the night before. "But something wonderful came out of all this. I found a love that would never let me down again."

"You met someone else?"

"Yes. Through my brother, I was re-introduced to Someone whose love is everlasting."

Julia suddenly realized that he was talking about Jesus Christ. Tears came to her eyes, seeing the look of utter sincerity on Adam's face.

He continued, "I've known about our Lord for years, but it took this crisis, this rejection, to make me see that I had basically never put Him first in my life. Suddenly, head knowledge was not enough. I had been a cerebral Christian, without the heart experience."

Julia got up, wiping her eyes quickly, and went to refill the coffee machine. Turning, she leaned against the sink. "It's strange, but tragedy seems to have brought you closer to the Lord." With a gesture of hopelessness, Julia whispered, "He seems so far away to me."

"He's there, Julia. Sometimes when we think He's the farthest away from us, He's the closest. Patrick and Marianne told me about Neal's death, and the great shock that you went through. Healing takes a while, Julia."

Adam looked down at Neal's note. "This unfortunately, has opened up the wounds again. It's strange how the same note if found the day Neal put it there would have brought you such pleasure... But finding it now..." Adam realized saying any more would only deepen the hurt.

Julia poured him some coffee, biting her lip and only being able to nod. She had prayed so often that the hurt would go away. Now she felt as if she were at square one again.

Sitting down with her cup of coffee before her, she whispered, "Thank you for being so understanding."

Adam sensed it was time to try to change the topic of conversation. "Our first plans have been changed for the day, but perhaps I could suggest something else?"

"Of course," Julia said, brushing away the tears that lingered on her cheeks.

Adam continued, "How about lunch, then the Metropolitan Museum—they have some Rembrandts and El Grecos there that I have been wanting to see for some time. I glanced at the *Times* and saw that Itzhak Perlman is playing Mendelssohn's violin concerto this evening at the Lincoln Center. Would that be something you'd enjoy?"

Julia smiled as she told him of wondering if he would like to go to the concert, when she had read about it in the morning newspaper. She never tired of visiting the Metropolitan . . .

"We seem to have some tastes in common," Adam said with delight. "Let me call and see if there could possibly be any tickets left."

Julia indicated the location of the telephone, and just as he exited from the kitchen, she turned to him and said, very quietly, "Thank you, Adam, for caring." Then she walked toward her bedroom to get her handbag.

Repairing her make up, she found that Adam's words were still ringing in her ears. "Sometimes when we think He's the farthest away from us, He's the closest."

I'll remember that, Lord, even though I don't feel Your nearness. . .I want to be able to feel You close to me once more.

She took her white wool scarf and hat, and went back to the kitchen to Adam.

"I forgot to mention that my parents would like us to come to dinner tomorrow night. They live out on Long Island, and I wondered if you would like to venture that far in this New York winter weather."

The smile on her face, and the white wool hat perched at a becoming angle over her raven black hair, made Julia look her enchanting self once more.

Adam said, admiring her with his eyes, "If you are willing to venture forth to Long Island, I'd be delighted. And. . .I have two tickets for the concert tonight!"

Julia clapped her hands, expressing her amazement and happiness. "They must have been cancellations."

"They were," Adam replied.

After a quick telephone call to her mother— who was more than pleased to hear Julia and her client would be coming the next day for dinner—Julia and Adam made their way to the renowned Metropolitan Museum.

•   •   •

Lunch was hardly exciting there, but Julia and Adam seemed not to notice. They found they had so much to talk about and she found him so easy to be with.

With a guide to the museum in her hands, they began their excursion through the treasures of the centuries.

At the top of the vast staircase leading to the section where the great masterpieces were housed was the awesome mural by Tiepolo—the eighteenth-century Italian painter. Adam and Julia craned their necks to look up at this magnificent eighteen-foot-high work of art.

Julia felt a twinge of excitement go through her. Inside this great building, where so much of man's agony and ecstasy had contributed to the arts, she sensed once more what all people have known—although often unexpressed, except through a painting or a sculpture: To love, and be loved. To find a reason for being. To be able to contribute something lasting for society, that might change for the better how mankind lives.

Adam's voice invaded her thoughts. "You, my dear friend, are miles away. These places have the same effect on me."

"I think it's the continuity of man's achievements through the years that always hits me. You see the same longings in them that we have today..."

Adam looked down at her and squeezed her arm. "There's a painting by El Greco I want to show you. Maybe you've seen it before."

They made their way slowly through the great rooms where paintings by Rubens, Vermeer, Rembrandt, and many others were displayed, until they arrived at the El Greco exhibit.

Adam led Julia over to the artist's interpretation of "The Miracle of Christ Healing the Blind Man."

"I've seen reproductions of it, but they don't capture the true colors or the compassion of Christ's face," Adam said reverently.

Julia stood looking at the painting, a sense of wonder in her eyes. "I've seen it before, but I have never quite identified with it as I do now. Perhaps I'm as blind as that man was—only in a different way. I need Jesus' healing too."

Adam put his arm around her shoulder. "It will come, Julia. It will come. Just give it time..."

Chapter
—5—

The concert at Lincoln Center had been glorious. Perlman's *joie de vivre*, and inspired playing of the Mendelssohn concerto had made the evening a particularly enjoyable one. Seated next to Adam, Julia had once more been conscious of the fact that he was a very attractive and masculine man. His nearness brought her comfort, yet there was an impelling excitement. . .

He had expressed how beautiful she looked. Julia had changed into a black velvet dress, with a white satin collar and matching cuffs.

Her lustrous black hair was caught up into a knot, and added to her regal appearance. Adam was quick to tell her how many people had noticed her entrance.

"You're embarrassing me, kind sir," she said with a lilt in her voice.

Julia was happy to be out once again. There had been so many evenings when she had refused people's offers of hospitality, and the agency was always getting first-night tickets. But somehow, without Neal, she had felt it all a waste of time.

Later, seated at a table at the Top of the Sixes" Restaurant on Fifth Avenue, Julia felt as if she were emerging from a self-imposed exile. She had suggested this restaurant because of the spectacular view, high above the glittering city of New York.

"I'm glad it's such a clear night for you, Adam."

He continued to gaze out of the window, watching the traffic ease its way up and down the Avenue. "Yes, it's a fantastic night." Then turning back to Julia, he said, "It's been a fantastic day. Thank you, Julia, for being willing to share this time with me."

His eyes gleamed in the candlelight, as he once more took in the beauty of her face. There was a lustrous sheen to her skin, and sparkle in her eyes that made her loveliness light up the darkly illuminated corner of the restaurant for Adam.

His attentive gaze made Julia begin discussing the concert once more. "I find that music has the same effect on me as art. There are moments that seem to transcend everyday living. It's hard to even express."

Adam continued to watch her, smiling as she used her hands to express herself.

The waiter arrived with their dessert—a delicate strawberry mousse, that melted in the mouth. Julia was grateful for the interruption. Before Adam could turn the conversation back to her, Julia boldly asked him, "Tell me about you. I mean your background—I hardly know anything about you except that you are from San Francisco, very successful, and you love El Greco and Mendelssohn!"

Adam laughed. It was evident that Julia was maneuvering the attention away from herself.

"You want to know from the very beginning?"

"From the very beginning. . ." Julia said, with mock gravity.

"Well, my background is very different than yours. My family was what you would call 'working-class.' We lived in the south of San Francisco in a very small row house, that my father walked out of one day, and to which he never returned."

"How devastating for your mother," Julia said, imagining the plight of Adam's family. "Have you never heard from him?"

"No, and I don't expect we ever will. Dad couldn't take the responsibility of a wife, and two small sons. When I was only six years old I remember hearing him tell my mother that we were a hindrance to him; that he was destined for far greater heights, and we were dragging him down."

Adam paused, and looked out of the window once more. "If it hadn't been for my mother and her belief in us, I often wonder what would have happened."

"She must be a very exceptional lady."

"She was. She died two years ago, and part of the sunshine went out of my life."

Julia said softly, "I'm sorry. I know what that feels like..."

Their eyes met and held—a sad smile was exchanged between them.

"But she left me with an inheritance that I shall cherish always. Her gentle example—her quiet faith. I'm thankful that for the last few years of her life, I was able to take care of her."

He looked out across the tops of the snow-laden skyscrapers. "She had never wanted a penthouse or a large estate, but she had often talked about perhaps one day owning a small condominium, overlooking the sea. Because my company became successful, I was able to grant her that wish. I shall always be grateful to the Lord that He made that possible."

Julia felt tears forming. "I wish I could have met her."

"She would have loved you. . . ." Adam said thoughtfully. Once more, Julia felt the dynamic intensity that was being transmitted between them.

"Does your brother live near you?"

"Yes, Tom lives out on the Peninsula. He's a minister, with a small church there. It was he who helped me see how much I was loved. . .after Georgina jilted me."

Julia was silent for a moment. She had never before met anyone quite like Adam. Yet, in many ways he reminded her of Neal. The same directness and honesty. There was a quiet strength about this handsomely disturbing man that she felt drawn to. . .

• • •

When she let herself into her apartment, later that night, Julia was thinking of their day

spent together. The visit to the Metropolitan,
the concert at the Lincoln Center, and then the
quiet candlelit dinner. It had been a marvel-
ous day, even though it had started out so
horrendously, with her finding Neal's note.

It now seemed days ago when she had found
it. But walking into the kitchen she saw the
piece of paper still on the table . . . a sorrowful,
silent reminder.

Beside it lay the open package containing the
gift Adam had bought her at the Metropolitan
Museum's gift shop. Julia opened it slowly to
look at it once more. It was a pure red, silk
crepe de chine scarf, its paisley design copied
from a Kashmir shawl.

Julia threw it around her neck, feeling the
soft texture against her cheek. She closed her
eyes and visualized Adam as he had said with
a quiet emphasis, "To remember our visit to
the Metropolitan, Julia."

He had taken her hand, and led her out of
the gift shop while she continued to thank
him for his thoughtfulness.

*Thank You, Lord, for bringing him into my
life. He's a very exceptional person . . .*

Julia thought again of the painting by El
Greco, and the expression on Christ's face as
He healed the blind man. She went to her
bedroom and, sitting on the bed, she found

the account of it in her Bible. She read once more of Jesus' compassion. Surely this loving Man could not have wished for Neal's death. Then why? Why was he taken at thirty-two, and why was there no peace in her heart?

Adam's words came back to her as they had stood looking at the painting, and she had admitted she needed healing also.

"It will come, Julia. It will come. Just give it time..."

Perhaps today has been a step toward finding it, she thought, hopefully.

• • •

The telephone awakened Julia early the next morning. It was Marianne calling from Connecticut, to tell her that she and Patrick would not be coming back into Manhattan until the evening after all.

"Can you cope with Adam, Julia? I'm sorry, but the reunion is going on longer than we thought."

Julia suddenly remembered she had invited Adam to Long Island for dinner, and had completely forgotten about Marianne and Patrick.

Relieved, she said, "Oh, I can manage fine, Marianne, I'm meeting him for church, and then after lunch we can go out to Long Island."

"How did yesterday go?" Marianne asked casually.

"Fine," Julia said, just as casually, "He's a very easy person to be with, and I'm sure that working with him is going to be a pleasure for all of us."

Marianne laughed. "Maybe more so for some of us? Patrick will be pleased when I tell him."

"Now don't go making more of this than is truthful. I have just enjoyed his company, and that, dear Marianne, is that." Julia tried to convey a slight severity in her tone, but realized she was unconvincing.

"Have a wonderful day with him, Julia, and try not to miss us too much!" Marianne said, laughingly.

"I'll try," she replied, laughing with her.

Julia put down the telephone, and glanced over at the scarf Adam had given her. She would wear it with her black wool suit and cape. She looked at her clothes hanging in the closet. There was a preponderance of black. Each time she had bought any clothes these last few months it seemed she automatically chose that color. With her striking coloring, and her skillful use of accessories, she always looked stunning. But today there was a certain dissatisfaction with her wardrobe.

A hat box caught her eye, high up in her
closet. It contained a hat she had not worn for
some time. A red felt, the perfect match for
Adam's scarf. Standing there in her night-
dress, she tried it on and spun around in front
of the mirror. The fedora shape comple-
mented her exquisite bone structure. She
decided it would be a lively completion to her
outfit—giving it the upbeat look that was
needed.

Julia looked at the clock by her bed. It was
still only 8:30 A.M. She had over two hours
before she had to meet Adam at her church.
She wished she were there now.

*I haven't felt like this, Lord, for so long.
Thank You for the gift of today.*

●   ●   ●

Adam was waiting on the steps of the
church when Julia's taxi arrived. She saw him
beating his hands together, trying to keep
warm as he watched for her. His handsome
face lit up with a radiant smile when he saw
her getting out of the taxi, and he ran down
the steps—insisting on paying for it.

"You look fabulous, Julia. What a knockout
of a hat!"

She laughed, explaining it had been stuck

on a shelf for months, and his scarf had
brought it back into service.

"They look great together."

He took her arm as they walked up the
steps, and they were welcomed enthusiastically by a deacon who knew Julia. Handing
them both the program for the order of service, the man expressed his pleasure in
meeting Julia's friend.

She was conscious that many people would
be staring at them today. It was the first time
she had been seen with a man since Neal's
death. Perhaps it had been a mistake to bring
Adam here. They should have gone to a
church where no one knew her.

Julia managed to smile at those she knew
as she walked with Adam down the aisle to
a vacant pew. Out of the corner of her eye she
saw Mrs. Cunningham raise her lorgnette—
trying to observe Julia's escort.

Julia caught her eye, and Mrs. Cunningham
disconcertedly put down her offending
glasses—trying to act as if she were not in the
least interested who was sitting next to Julia.
A dropped hymn book added to Mrs. Cunningham's confusion.

The organist was playing the introit, and the
music filled the vast church. The sounds of
the familiar music brought tears to Julia's eyes,

but she knew it was part of the necessary heartache on the road she now travelled without Neal.

Accepting it is part of the healing process, she thought.

Adam turned to look at her as they stood together to sing the first hymn. There was a wealth of understanding in his eyes.

O Love that will not let me go,
I rest my weary soul in thee. . .

Chapter
—6—

For Julia, the drive out to Long Island was filled with mixed emotions. Adam had volunteered to drive her car, and now, speeding toward her family's estate, she kept visualizing Neal sitting in the driver's seat. How many times they had driven to Long Island together—discussing business, or where they would go to completely unwind after a hectic week at the agency.

During their last summer together they had spent ten glorious days in Bermuda, fascinated with the unspoiled British island and its proud traditions. Long walks along the sun-drenched beaches had helped to calm the jarred nerves, that were par for the course in advertising. Swimming, riding, and sailing together had made the vacation almost too perfect.

I should have known it was too wonderful to last, she thought.

Julia watched the snow-laden countryside flash by, and became conscious once more of Adam's presence. Turning to him apologetically, she said, "Please forgive me. I'm not being a very good guide to Long Island for you."

"I know your thoughts have been far away, Julia," Adam said understandingly.

She looked down at her gloves, and pulling them tighter over her fingers, she said, "It's always hard to come back. Neal and I spent a great deal of time out here." Biting her lip, Julia continued, "It's so strange how just a small thing can trigger a memory. Imagine, in spite of the snow I was remembering a vacation we had spent in Bermuda!"

"I do the very same thing, Julia, whenever I'm somewhere that Georgina or I have been together."

They drove along silently for a few minutes, through country lanes that would soon bring them to their destination.

"Did you ever go to San Francisco with

Neal?" Adam asked quietly.

"No. We were always talking about spending some time there." There was a note of regret in Julia's voice.

"Then perhaps your trip to the West Coast will be helpful to you."

"I hope so. But even as I say that I feel guilty, thinking that I might enjoy being somewhere without Neal."

Julia turned to look at Adam, and he smiled sadly, looking straight ahead at the road.

"Don't be, Julia. Neal would want you to be happy. You have to go on living—making new associations, visiting new places."

"I know," she said, almost inaudibly. Then she realized they were almost to the gates of her parents' home. "Oh, sorry . . . you have to turn left here."

Adam stopped in time and turned the car into the long drive that led them to a large, red brick mansion. Switching off the engine, he looked up at the house.

"It's beautiful, Julia. Don't you ever miss it, cooped up in Manhattan?"

"Sometimes. But I don't miss all the responsibilities that go with it," she said with determination.

"Such as?"

"The social scene. I'm afriad I've always

been the bane of my mother's life. She should have had another daughter—one who would enter into all the seemingly necessary involvement in committees, tea parties to discuss where the next committee meeting should be held, et cetera, et cetera!"

Adam laughed. "I take it you have not often been a willing participant in any of your mother's plans?"

"Hardly."

As they walked up the pathway to the house, they noticed that the wind was increasing again. "It's coming straight off the ocean, so it feels even colder," Julia shouted, leading Adam into the house.

The large, stately hall, with its marble floor and impressive, grand staircase, made Julia's voice echo as she called for her mother and father.

"It must be siesta time for both of them," Julia said confidentially, smiling up at Adam. "A family tradition for Sunday afternoon. Read the newspapers and fall asleep. Let me take your coat. Mother always gives the staff off after Sunday luncheon. Very democratic, don't you think?"

"Very. But then I wouldn't know about dealing with servants, remember?" Adam smiled at her. "I'm from the working class."

Julia smiled back at him, thinking how very much she was enjoying his unpretentious company. Flinging open the double doors, which led to the large, elegant living room, she invited him in. A tray set for tea had been placed on a low table by the fire.

"Please—do sit down. I'll go and make us some tea." She bent down to pick up the silver teapot from the tray.

Adam sat down on an enormous, pale turquoise sofa, which was opposite an equally enormous companion. "That sounds good, Julia. Your Long Island weather has chilled me to the bone."

Crossing the hall, Julia walked quickly down the corridor leading to the kitchen. Just then her mother came running down the stairs.

"Julia! I'm so sorry I wasn't down to greet your guest. Where is he?"

Lorraine Taylor was still trying to fix her hair, when Julia pointed to the living room.

"Mother, please, try not to scare him away. He's a good client—nothing else."

Mrs. Taylor looked back at Julia, with an incredulous expression. "How silly of you, Julia. As if I would presume anything else."

Lorraine Taylor was still a very attractive woman in her early fifties. She carried herself regally, and Julia had inherited her jet black hair and striking good looks. Her mother walked hurriedly toward the living room. Julia watched her for a few seconds, wanting to go with her to spare Adam any embarrassment, but then she remembered the tea.

The kettle took so long to boil, or so it seemed. Julia finally returned to the living room to find her mother and Adam deep in conversation. He was laughing about an incident that had happened to Julia when she was a child.

"So you see, we have always been very proud of Julia, even though there have been those times when she has not behaved quite as she should," Mrs. Taylor concluded.

"Whatever are you telling Adam?" Julia asked, placing the silver teapot down on the tray, and pretending to be annoyed.

"I was telling him about the time we had all those terribly important people for tea, and you decided to ride your bicycle right through this room—knocking over a table of sandwiches and cakes on to the lap of an irate, rather large lady!"

"Mother, I was only five years old at the time."

"And so adorable, Julia. I really miss those days." Lorraine Taylor's dark brown eyes clouded over for a moment. "We hardly ever get to see her now, Mr. Kingsley. She's so busy at the agency, dreaming up new ways to lure the public to buy products. Is that why you are in New York?"

"Yes, it is. Well, partly. I'm also on a few days' vacation."

Mrs. Taylor drew a deep sigh. "What a time to come to New York. This is hardly vacation weather."

"No, but your daughter has helped to make my visit very special." Adam glanced over at Julia, and her mother was quick to notice the look exchanged between them.

"It's a pleasure, Adam, to show you a little of our local scenery." Julia was trying not to let her mother see that she was attracted to this impellingly handsome man. But nothing escaped Lorraine Taylor's inquisitive, discerning eyes.

She noticed how radiant her daughter looked today. The red silk scarf thrown casually around her neck, added to the relaxed and joyous look that had been missing for so long.

Julia passed Adam a plate of pastries, refusing one herself. "I'm thinking ahead to dinner. Mother always has the most incredible selection on Sunday evenings. She calls it her Buffet de Taylor."

"Julia, don't raise Mr. Kingsley's hopes. After all, it is only a cold buffet, except for the soup, because the cook has the evening off," her mother quickly responded.

"I'm sure it will be delicious, Mrs. Taylor. By the way, do please call me Adam."

"But of course, thank you." The ormolu clock on the ornately carved mantlepiece chimed five o'clock and Lorraine Taylor rose to her feet.

"If you will excuse me, I will take some tea up to my husband. Julia, why don't you show Adam the house? I'm sorry the weather is so unsuitable for her to show you the grounds. Dinner will be at 7:30, so I know Julia can amuse you until then."

Adam had risen to his feet and watched while the elegant, high-powered woman left—balancing a teacup and a small plate of sandwiches and cake for her husband. "He's extremely tired today. The rally on Wall Street this week absolutely exhausted him, poor dear."

Julia and Adam smiled at each other... There were a few moments of awkward silence, then Julia asked him, "Would you like to see the rest of the house?"

"Yes, I would, but first tell me about this

room. The paintings and paneling are really magnificent." Adam walked over to the fireplace and ran his hands over the carved mantlepiece.

"Well, most of the paneling, and the mantle, came from England. My parents bought them in an auction. An old manor house was being converted by its new owners, who didn't care too much for antiques." Julia suddenly stopped. "Now, come to think of it, the name of the old house was Kingsley Manor. Who knows—it could have been owned by your ancestors!"

"That's a nice thought, but highly unlikely."

"But Kingsley is a very English name, isn't it?"

"Yes, but I've never heard anything about my forebears. Dad leaving us, when I was so young, kind of put an end to all that. Mother really didn't mention any relatives on Dad's side of the family."

"It's still a fascinating possibility, and I'd love to do some digging for you. There are agencies in England which will trace your heritage," Julia said excitedly.

"I knew someone once who did that, only to find out that one of his ancestors was a highwayman!" Adam said gravely, with a twinkle in his eye.

"How very romantic."

"Romantic? I think of that word as conjuring up love—idealistic, perfect." Adam moved closer to Julia and she felt her heart skip a beat.

"Well, I was thinking of the romance of that period of history. Men on horses, rescuing maidens in distress—riding off with them to a life of perfect bliss." She stepped back from him, and raising her eyes to the ceiling to change the subject began to point out the beautiful mouldings and the magnificent chandelier.

"This came from France, from a chateau outside of Paris."

"It's very lovely, but then so is everything in this room." Adam was not looking at the chandelier, or the room. His eyes were riveted on Julia.

"Well, thank you." She felt her cheeks burn, and hastily she turned away from his disturbing gaze.

Feeling unsure of herself, Julia took him on a grand tour of the house. Fortunately, in the library, Adam found some first editions of Pascal that intrigued him for awhile—but Julia realized that the chemistry between them was becoming more and more apparent.

Walking up the stairs, Adam said, "I can just visualize you as a little girl here . . . what a fabulous house to grow up in."

"Yes, it was. But it was sometimes very lonely. Being an only child, I had to amuse myself quite often."

"My childhood was the opposite. With my brother I sometimes wished for some peace!"

They were nearing Julia's old room, and she asked if he would like to see it.

"Oh, yes," he answered jokingly. "I can see where so much of your character was formed."

Julia opened a door which led into a large, bright bedroom. The walls were covered in a softly colored, floral wallpaper—a perfect background for the single four-poster bed, with hangings of white lace. Dainty Georgian tables and a lady's writing desk added to the feeling of quiet elegance and serenity.

A large bay window overlooked the vast gardens, and Julia and Adam walked over to look down at the rural beauty, clothed in a dense blanket of snow.

"It was from down there that a helicopter arrived to whisk Neal and me off on our honeymoon . . . it all seems so long ago now."

Julia turned back to look at her old room. "So many of my plans and dreams were thought out here," she said wistfully and walked over to a small table by her bed.

Picking up a well-worn New Testament, Julia said, "Mother and Father gave this to me, when I was only seven years old."

She fanned through the pages, and showed Adam her childish handwriting on so many of the margins. "You can see, I was fortunate enough to have had a childhood that gave me something to cling to as I grew up."

"Yes, and something to go on fortifying you today, Julia," Adam said calmly. "Those words don't change, whatever our circumstances. God's love for us is as real today as when you first received that Testament."

Julia thought for a moment, and then said quietly, "I know. I just have to find it again, that's all."

"It's there, it has never left you, Julia. Remember what Jesus said shortly before He died. 'Lo, I am with you always, even unto the end of the world'? That means exactly what He said, *always*."

Julia smiled up at him. "Thank you again, for being so understanding. I am beginning to feel my life is not so hopeless any more."

She walked back to the window and whispered, "How often I would sit here and think if only I had been born somewhere else, in a different era, under different circumstances, then everything would be perfect. It was only the *now* that made everything wrong." Julia laughed apologetically. "I must have been a very introspective child. I make it sound as if I were never happy. I was. But there were times when I longed to live in a small row house, and to be able to be part of the teeming world out there."

"And I often longed to be able to get away from my noisy row house, and live in the country!" Adam continued, "But now I realize it isn't your circumstances that are the most important part of your life. Each one of us has access to the Power that can change our whole being—wherever we live or find ourselves."

"You mean Jesus Christ?"

Adam nodded. "Only He can make us new again, Julia. He picks up the broken pieces of our lives, and restores them. He's still restoring mine—each day I feel stronger. The hurt doesn't destroy me any more."

He put his arm around Julia's shoulder, and the warmth of him standing so close made her turn to him. She rested her head against his broad chest.

Tears were running down her cheeks, but they were tears of joy.

"I'm beginning to see, Adam, that my life didn't end when Neal died. God does still love me . . ."

Chapter
—7—

The "Buffet de Taylor" was a great success. Steaming hot clam chowder gave a hearty start to the otherwise cold buffet.

In the kitchen, while Julia helped her mother with all the last-minute preparations for dinner, Mrs. Taylor had told her how much she approved of Adam.

"He's really charming, Julia. I wonder if you'd like me to check up on his family for you?"

"Don't you *dare*, Mother. And please, don't embarrass me at dinner." Julia had seen that

her mother was being her obvious matchmaking self. "I told you he's just a client of
mine."

Mrs. Taylor had smiled, as she ladled out the
clam chowder. "And when do 'just clients'
hug, may I ask? I passed by your door and saw
his arms around you." Seeing Julia's annoyed
expression, she had swiftly added, "I was on
my way downstairs—not prying, mind you,
or anything like that."

Seated now at the table opposite Adam, Julia
remembered the warmth of his arms around
her. He looked up and, noticing she was looking at him, winked. Instead of feeling mor-
tified, remembering how Neal had always
done that, Julia felt her face glow.

Her father was asking Adam about his computer business, telling him he was sure he
could introduce him to several key companies
that would be more than interested in this
product. Julia watched her father. How he
loved to be able to help anyone. His face was
animated as he talked about the future Adam
had.

"What a time for you to be in the business
of manufacturing computers. It's a vast, growing market. Julia, you have a very interesting
client here."

"I know, Father," and in spite of herself, she

laughed softly. Her face reddened slightly when she caught Adam's amused look.

Julia sensed that her mother was dying to say something pointed, but instead she merely asked Adam if he wouldn't like to return to the buffet.

"Please do. There will be so much left over. I forgot that Julia is on a perpetual diet."

"So are you," James Taylor called out. "She sneaks things though, when she thinks no one is around. I've caught her with an enormous bowl of ice cream—furtively creeping up the back stairs to a vacant guest room!"

"Absolutely nonsense, James. You do exaggerate. You saw me once with a very *small* bowl of diet ice cream. I hadn't wanted to disturb you."

Adam went over to the buffet, and once more piled his plate with the delicious offerings that had been prepared.

"I'll have to get Julia to take me for a run around Central Park after this. It's really excellent food, Mrs. Taylor."

"I'm glad you are enjoying it, Adam. It's a pleasure to have you in our home." Lorraine Taylor looked quickly at Julia. "Will you two be flying to San Francisco together?" she asked casually.

Julia said quietly, "I hadn't even thought

about it," and avoided Adam's eyes.

"I had. I think it would be a wonderful idea," Adam said enthusiastically. "Long flights are so boring, and your sparkling company would help the time to slip by."

She smiled at him, thinking how pleasant it would be to travel with him . . .

"Did you call Alexandra, Julia?" her mother asked.

"I completely forgot!"

"How very unlike you. You don't usually forget things. You must have had a *great* deal on your mind. Why don't you call her after dinner?"

"Yes, Mother, I will." Looking at Adam, Julia said, "I had thought I would leave for San Francisco next Wednesday."

"That sounds fine with me. I should be able to wrap up all my business here by then," Adam said approvingly.

After dinner, Julia telephoned Alexandra Panov. She sounded a little hesitant about Julia staying with her. The room she could offer Julia was very small . . . Julia assured her that she would not be in it very much. Working, sight-seeing—and in her mind, being with Adam quite often—would not leave her a great deal of time. Finally, it was agreed she would stay.

When Julia put the telephone down, she thought how frail Alexandra's voice had sounded, even though she had said she was fine. Gone was the strong, vivacious welcome she had always received before. Perhaps she was ill. Julia was puzzled. Yet, she sensed Alexandra would be pleased to see her.

• • •

The first part of the drive back to Manhattan was spent mostly in silence. Julia was perfectly comfortable with it, and she felt Adam was too. Later, he told her how much he had enjoyed meeting her parents. He said they had made him feel welcome, and he was not ill at ease with them at all—in spite of the difference in their backgrounds.

"Why should you be, Adam? I have always failed to see why there should be any barrier because of money." Julia stretched out her legs and leaned her head back. "I've rather resented my roots. But then perhaps I'm not as grateful as I should be for my heritage."

"Perhaps you're not." It was a blunt statement, but Adam's voice had a tender tone. "The more God blesses me though the more I realize how much I owe to others. It was my knowledge in technology that started it all, but I have to rely on other people to carry it on."

"You think I'm a poor little rich girl?" Julia asked, rather defensively.

"Not at all. But I think because your family is wealthy, you've carried a guilt complex around with you for a long time."

Julia thought for a few seconds. "I guess you're right. I have." After the initial shock of being confronted in such a direct way by Adam, she smiled. "It's not every day a man analyzes me in such a charming way."

"I didn't mean to sound like your local psychiatrist, forgive me."

Adam realized he had to turn on to the Long Island Expressway, back to Manhattan, and during these few moments Julia studied him closely.

The headlights of other cars illuminated his face. He had a rugged, distinctive profile that Julia found very attractive. Adam had touched on something that had bothered her for so long—her wealth—and he had been completely matter-of-fact about it. She decided she liked his forthright manner.

"Analyzing *me* now?" Adam asked, conscious of her intent gaze. He turned momentarily to smile at her, then his attention went back to the freeway.

"In a way. But I was thinking you are the first person to really confront me with one of my nagging concerns."

Julia looked out of the window. "As a Christian, how do I accept the fact that I have so much more than many others?"

"I am facing the same question now. After so many years of living beneath the poverty level as a child, I now find myself among the rich. I, too, feel the responsibility of it all. When God trusts us with money, He also requires us to be good stewards of His gifts."

"I know. Oh, I tithe, but it never seems to be enough somehow."

"Perhaps He needs more of our time," Adam said thoughtfully. "I know I don't give Him nearly enough. I keep saying I will when this project is finished, or that problem is resolved...but then something else turns up to take my attention."

"That's what has happened to me. My hospital visitation work that the church sponsors, will have to be put aside while I go on this trip to San Francisco," Julia said, allowing her frustration to show.

"My brother, who has a church on the Peninsula, will be glad to keep you busy. He has a drug rehabilitation program for young people that constantly needs volunteers to counsel them."

"I'd like to help them while I'm there," Julia said thoughtfully. "Some of my friends have almost been destroyed by drugs."

She was thinking of Patrick in particular. Last year Neal had received a telephone call in the middle of the night from Marianne. Patrick had been to a late night party, given by one of his top clients—cocaine had been passed around, and he had taken some. From then on he was hooked on it, and Marianne told Neal she could see it was ruining the once strong, endearing man she had married.

With love and prayer, Neal had finally been able to help Patrick. The wonder of it all was that through all the heartache, Marianne and Patrick had given their lives to the Lord.

It was these two dear friends who had helped Julia that devastating day Neal had died . . .

The glittering skyline of Manhattan came into view—a reminder to Julia that the weekend was almost over.

"Tomorrow we shall begin working on your big promotional program. I'm really looking forward to it, Adam."

"So am I." He reached out and squeezed her hand. "Little did I know, when I engaged Fraser and Marshall as my advertising agents,

I would be working with the beautiful Julia Marshall."

Adam's hand remained on Julia's, and she rested her other hand on top of it. It felt so natural to her. So much of the lonelines of the past ten months seemed to be swept away sitting beside him. Julia thought of the way his presence next to her in church had added to the feeling of contentment she now felt.

Reluctantly, Adam took his hand away and concentrated on driving through the brightly lit, teeming streets of the city, until they arrived at Julia's apartment building. He drove down to the underground garage, and switched off the engine of her car.

Handing back the keys, he said, "Thank you for another wonderful day, Julia. I've enjoyed being with you so much."

"Thank you," she whispered, starting to walk toward the elevator. "I've really enjoyed it too."

Adam punched the lobby and the 10th floor buttons, which Julia was quick to notice.

"Wouldn't you like to have a quick cup of coffee?"

"I don't think I should . . ."

Adam stepped closer to Julia and straightened the red silk scarf that he had bought at the Metropolitan Museum.

His eyes searched hers, and for one moment she thought he would bend down and kiss her.

The elevator doors opened, and with an almost brusque, "Good night, Julia, I'll see you tomorrow," Adam was gone.

She leaned her head against the elevator, feeling it vibrate as it ascended to her floor. Julia remembered the exciting sensation she felt of the touch of Adam's fingers on her neck, while he straightened her scarf—the look of burning intensity in his eyes. . .

The elevator doors opened, and Julia walked quickly to her apartment. Entering, she quickly shut the door and walked down the hall to her bedroom. Flinging the red fedora hat onto the pristine white Early American quilt on the four-poster bed, she turned and looked at herself in the mirror.

Gone was the haunted look of sorrow that had pervaded her velvety brown eyes. A radiance had invaded her. Her expression was one of hope and expectation. Perhaps there was a bright future for her after all . . . she had tomorrow to look forward to. . . .

The door bell rang three times. Whoever was there was very insistent.

Julia walked quickly to the door and anxiously called out, "Who is it?"

"Adam."

Julia's heart skipped a beat. Opening the door, she looked up at him, and smiled...her eyes revealing her pleasure.

"Hi," Adam said, in his low and husky voice.

"Hi," Julia replied, breathlessly.

Adam suddenly swept her up in his arms and kissed her—his lips searching hers. The passion Julia felt swept her completely away for a few blissful seconds, then Adam released her very abruptly.

Before Julia knew what was happening, Adam was striding back to the elevator.

"See you tomorrow..." and he was gone.

She closed the door to her apartment, still reeling from the impact of his kiss.

"See you, Adam," she whispered.

Monday morning would not be something to dread—she would be seeing him, and the thought made her smile. She took off the red silk scarf and ran it across her cheek... remembering his kiss.

Chapter
—8—

Fraser and Marshall's streamlined offices, on the 24th floor of the Chase Building, were teeming with staff, clients, and frustrated artists—all involved in launching three major campaigns. Advertising for baby food, cars, and Adam's computers was all being readied to persuade the American public that these products were far superior to any of their rivals.

Julia sat at her desk trying to answer the telephone, and at the same time giving instructions to her secretary about some top priority decisions that had to be made immediately. She hastily dictated a letter to an ancestry research company in England, asking them to trace Adam's possible connection to Kingsley Manor.

Her mind was not completely on her work, knowing that any moment Adam would be walking into her office. Despite the somber, gray light of another snow-filled morning, Julia imagined that if she looked out of the window down onto Madison Avenue, she would see that spring had arrived. The thought of Adam had that effect on her. . . .

Patrick put his head around the door and called out, "Pick up line two—it's the San Francisco office wanting to make arrangements about your trip."

Julia picked up the telephone and proceeded to talk with their man in charge of the agency, Bob Coleman. No, she would not need anyone to meet her, or a hotel. Yes, she was looking forward to being there, too. Julia's head was bent over her desk; her lustrous black hair falling over her eyes obstructed the view of the door. Standing there, watching in admiration was Adam. . . .

Julia put down the telephone, and swung around in her chair to look for an appointment book. Startled, she realized Adam was

standing there. She looked up into his disturb-
ingly captivating eyes. The self-assured career
woman was gone. Julia found herself fighting
for composure as he walked toward her desk.

"Hi, Julia. I now see you in your official surroundings. I'm very impressed." He leaned forward, and said confidentially, "You look just
as beautiful. . .before we even start talking
advertising, may I ask if you'll have lunch
with me?"

Julia pushed back her hair, and began
straightening the papers on her desk so she
would not have to keep looking at him. "I'd
like that. . . . Yes, thank you."

She had chosen carefully the camel-colored,
fine wool suit, that gave her an authoritative
air—but had substituted the cream silk
tailored shirt she usually wore with it, for a
softly feminine, eggshell blue blouse that ruffled flatteringly around her neck and wrists.
Pearls added a chic, tasteful touch.

Julia got up and walked over to a long table
by her window, piled high with masses of
files, layouts, and photographs.

Clearing her throat, she said, "Adam, here
are some of the suggested layouts that our
artists have come up with. Of course, these
are only in the rough stages and we'll need
to go over these together at some length."

Adam stood beside her and in a low voice responded, "I'm so glad."

Julia shed her businesslike attitude and laughed. "I can see it's not going to be easy working on this project, Mr. Kingsley, unless you really concentrate completely on the business at hand. . . ."

He said, "I agree with you, but you do make it difficult for a man to keep his mind on computers!"

Julia took a few steps away from him. "Patrick will be joining us soon, so perhaps it will be easier." Julia wanted to say, "For both of us," but she withheld, knowing Adam would read even more into her feelings.

The memory of his kiss that had surprised her late last night at her front door, now came back to send a shock wave of emotion running through her. Mercifully, Patrick came into the room, and they began to discuss the appropriate strategy to launch the sale of Adam's computers nationwide.

●　●　●

Seated at a table for two in a small, French restaurant on Madison Avenue, Julia found herself relaxing once more with Adam. In the setting of the agency, it was hard to

disassociate him from the friend/client relationship. She also found it difficult, with the
staff around her, not to think of Neal. They
had worked together on so many campaigns.
He would have known instinctively the
perfect approach to use, and so often she
found herself thinking, "What would Neal
have done. . .?"

"I keep saying to myself that somehow you
don't really belong in this cutthroat world of
advertising," Adam said, in a tone that
reflected his admiration for this beautiful
young woman who amazed him with her
gentleness on the one hand, and her brilliant
business prowess on the other.

"It certainly is cutthroat. The competition
is fierce, and if I felt that this were the only
thing that was important to me, I would probably have had a nervous breakdown long
ago!"

The waiter brought their coffee, while
Julia thought for a moment, then she continued, "Perhaps what haunts me the most
is the influence that the advertising world
has on society. Our agency tries not to accept
accounts we feel are contrary to our beliefs.
It's not easy to turn down an account, because, as you said, the whole business is
so ruthless. But Patrick and I believe we

can't compromise our faith."

"That's why God honors you both..."
Adam said quietly.

"After Neal died, I went through a great
deal of soul searching about whether I should
continue with the agency. It was different
somehow when I was merely working there,
but when I took over the partnership all the
tremendous decisions were suddenly left up
to Patrick and me. I found it hard to keep trying to win new clients. I still do." Julia shrugged and gave an apologetic smile.

"You won me over the first moment I saw
you."

Julia smiled again. "Patrick netted you
before you even met me!" She stirred her coffee, thinking of their first meeting.

"But I was more than delighted when he
released me to you!" Adam said, gazing into
her eyes.

Julia quickly thought of an old adage that
would take the attention away from her. "Do
you remember Emerson's statement that is
still so up-to-date, and applies to an excellent
product—like yours?"

Adam shook his head. "I can't think of it
offhand."

Julia quoted, "If a man has good corn, or

wood, or boards, or pigs to sell, or can make
better chairs, or knives, or crucibles, or
church organs, than anybody else, you will
find a broad, hard beaten road to his house,
though it be in the woods!"

"May the road be easier to find my computers!" Adam paused, his head on one side.
"You know, it does sound familiar. I must
have read it in college..." He stopped
abruptly.

Julia noticed that Adam was watching a tall,
attractive, blonde young woman walk by and
exit out of the restaurant. His eyes had
clouded, and for a moment he seemed
unaware of Julia's presence.

Adam saw the apprehension reflected in
Julia's eyes. "I'm sorry, Julia. Forgive me. For
a moment I thought it was Georgina, my ex-
fiancee."

He signaled the waiter for more coffee. It
was apparent that seeing the young woman
had disturbed him. Instinctively, Julia knew
what he was going through.

"I often think I see Neal. I'll see him going
through a revolving door of a hotel, or when
I'm walking down the street, I think, 'There
he is, just a few people ahead of me,' and I find
myself quickening my pace. Then the knowledge hits me once more—I'll never see him

walking down any of these streets again."

Tears were beginning to form in her eyes, and she was angry with herself for sharing this with Adam. Right now, he didn't need to hear about her loss. His had so unsettled him.

Julia felt Adam's hand on hers. "It's only a natural reaction, isn't it? It will pass, but we have to accept these situations as being normal." He laughed hollowly. "I must say, whoever that young woman was, she really shook me up for a few moments."

"Tell me about Georgina, Adam. How long had you known her?"

"For several years. We met while I was attending Stanford University, and from the first date we both knew that was it. Neither of us ever looked at anyone else, until. . ." Adam clenched his jaw. "Well, until she went to Europe. She met someone she felt would make her happier, I guess."

"Were you very compatible, before that?" Julia asked softly.

"In many ways, but our courtship was quite a roller coaster. I never knew what mood would hit her. Actually, we often seemed to bring out the worst in each other."

"Then perhaps God spared both of you a lot of future heartache," Julia said quietly, thinking of the idyllic marriage she had experienced with Neal.

"I'm sure He did. I only hope she will be happy with whoever she met in France." The sad smile Julia had seen so often, lingered on Adam's face.

Reluctantly, Julia looked at her watch and saw that they had taken well over an hour for lunch. "I really must be getting back to the agency. I have mountains of work to get done before I leave with you on Wednesday."

Adam apologetically rose to his feet. "Forgive me for keeping you like this. Especially for dragging up my past."

"I asked you to tell me about it, remember? Anyway, you have helped me so much. I find each time I mention Neal now, it's easier for me. The healing *is* slow, but it's working."

Julia touched his arm, and her warmth and sensitivity made Adam seem to want to kiss her again. She turned her face away, knowing how very much she wanted to respond. . .

Walking back up Madison Avenue, Adam took her arm and Julia thought how much she was looking forward to San Francisco.

She turned to look up at him, and he put his arm around her shoulder and gave her a hug.

"Julia, only two more days, and I'll be showing you my hometown. I can't wait!"

Impulsively, Julia exclaimed, "Neither can I!"

Chapter
—9—

The flight to San Francisco seemed to have gone by so quickly for Julia. She could hardly believe that in just a few minutes the plane would be landing. The hostess announced that the weather was a mild 60 degrees and raining.

"Naturally," laughed Adam. "I'm glad you brought your raincoat."

Julia had rushed into Bloomingdale's, before leaving New York, and purchased a new one. Automatically she had reached for a black, very stylish raincoat—then seeing a bright red one, she had tried it on and decided to purchase it. She was tired of black. It was a constant reminder of the past.

Adam had remarked how attractive the raincoat was. The back had a flare to it, which moved gracefully as Julia walked. The upturned collar framed her exquisite face, and made her feel more alive.

The plane landed and Adam helped her into the raincoat, whispering, "You're going to light up the streets of San Francisco, Julia Marshall!"

She laughed, and taking down the matching umbrella from the overhead compartment, she said, "It looks as if I'm going to get a great deal of use out of my latest purchases."

Adam quickly escorted her out of the plane, and down to the baggage area. While the carousel seemed to go endlessly around without any trace of their bags on it, Julia's thoughts were on Alexandra Panov. She had her address written down, and asked Adam if he knew where Alexandra's street was.

He looked at the piece of paper, and a slow smile came over his face. "Believe it or not, it's two blocks from where I lived as a boy."

"Really?"

"Yes, it's in South San Francisco."

"How strange. I thought it would be somewhere in the center of the city near her work." Julia saw one of her suitcases come into view, and Adam went to retrieve it. Thoughtfully, she said, "It means I'll have to rent a car. Why don't I go and get one while you wait for the luggage?"

Adam was taking a taxi. He had told her he would give her directions to Alexandra's and then go on to the Wharf, where he had a condominium in a high-rise overlooking the Bay. Now, Julia realized the area she would be staying in was not going to be very convenient for her. But the thought of seeing Alexandra Panov again dispelled any regrets.

Finally, Julia's rental car was ready for her, and with her luggage safely stowed in the trunk, she reluctantly said "Au revoir" to Adam.

"I'll call you later tonight," he said, kissing her gently on the lips. "I shall miss you 'til then, my beautiful friend."

His kiss intensified Julia's sadness at leaving him. She drove out of the airport feeling strangely alone...realizing how much his presence had grown to mean to her.

The freeway was crowded with rush hour traffic, but luckily most of it seemed to be going the other way. Adam had sketched a quick map, showing exactly where Alexan-

dra's street was, and before long Julia pulled
up outside her house. She turned off the
engine of the car, and looked up at it. The
paint was peeling, and the steps leading up
to the front door were crumbling and badly
in need of repair.

Julia glanced at the paper with Alexandra's
address on it again. Surely this was not the
right house? Julia remembered the elegant
home in Bronxville that she had often visited:
the immaculate garden, with the brick path
leading up to the equally immaculate front
door. The feeling of welcome she had always
experienced flashed through her mind.

Julia looked up at the house once more, and
noticed that a tattered lace curtain in one of
the windows moved slightly—as if someone
were watching her. Julia decided she should
get out of the car and see if this were the right
address.

A few minutes went by until she heard
footsteps, and the sound of the door being
opened. Alexandra stood there, and Julia
fought back the tears, as she saw what only
two years had done to this beautiful woman.
She was in her early fifties, yet she looked
years older.

The jet black hair, drawn back in typical
ballerina style, was now tinged with gray.

Alexandra's face was pale and lined—her eyes looked painfully sad, yet there was an expression of pleasure in them as she welcomed Julia.

The two women hugged, and Julia felt the frailness of this dear friend. Leading her down the small hallway, Alexandra apologized for the state of the little house.

"It's rather difficult for me to manage these days."

Julia noticed she walked with the aid of a silver topped cane. Even though it was difficult for Alexandra to maneuver she still walked with the elegance of a ballerina.

Leading Julia into her small living room, Alexandra motioned for her to be seated, as she herself sank down onto an armchair by the fireplace, where a small fire was burning.

Julia looked quickly around the room, recognizing some of the furniture that Alexandra had brought from her Bronxville home. It looked incongruous against the background of walls that needed repapering, and a carpet that was threadbare.

"Now you know why I was hesitant about you staying with me, Julia," Alexandra said sadly.

Julia went over to her and knelt down, putting her arms around the frail shoulders. They did not speak for a few moments, then Julia

whispered, "Have you been ill, Alexandra?"
She nodded.

"Tell me what happened."

"I had a stroke. The doctor said it was
brought on by shock." Alexandra turned to
look into the fire, tears in her eyes. "I learned
that after all these years of hoping to be
reunited with my husband, he had died in
Russia—in a slave-labor camp."

"Alexandra!" Julia cried out in disbelief.
"I'm so sorry. But why did you never tell us?"

"Because at the same time, I lost all my
money. I had trusted someone with it who felt
that I should invest it all in a new project. The
project failed, and I wound up with nothing.
I just had to get away from New York and try
to begin again. Then I had a stroke, and now
you see the nearly empty shell of your former
friend."

"Don't say that, Alexandra. We'll always be
friends, whatever the circumstances. Did you
really think that money would make the difference in our friendship?"

"Perhaps my pride didn't want you to see
me like this." Tears ran down her cheeks. "I
suppose God has had to teach me humility the
hard way . . ."

"He doesn't send us sorrow, but sometimes
He allows it, Alexandra, so we can see how

much we really must depend on Him." Julia thought of her loss of Neal. At least she knew that everything was done to save him. Alexandra did not have that comfort. "Wherever your husband died, he was not alone. Remember that, Alexandra. Our Lord was with him. You told me once how much he loved to read his Bible, and how he had told you of his love for Jesus Christ."

Looking at this tragically beautiful woman, Julia remembered how Alexandra had met her husband while she was in Russia performing with her ballet company. They had fallen in love and after a great deal of apprehension he was granted a visa to come to the United States. They married and lived in New York, where he established himself in the publishing business. They had been exceptionally happy, until the year he decided to go back to Russia to see his mother. He was never allowed out of the country again. Alexandra had pined for him for over fifteen years. Now, she knew he was dead.

Julia felt heartbroken for Alexandra. "I'm so thankful I came out here. Things are going to be different for you. Mother will want to have you stay with her, if you feel well enough to travel."

"Oh, no, I couldn't be a burden to her, Julia.

She has so much charity work to attend to. . .I would be in her way."

"Charity is supposed to begin in the home. You're family to us, and I refuse to think of you having to live alone. You need someone to take care of you. Have you had anything to eat today?"

"Oh, yes, Julia, don't worry about me. I have a young girl who comes in and does a little housework and shops for me. But what about yourself?" She smiled. "There's a delicious TV dinner in the freezer, if you'd like that! I pretend when I eat them I'm dining in one of my favorite restaurants in New York. Dressed in silks and satins, and among my old friends. It helps make them taste just a little better, Julia."

Julia laughed with her, glad to see Alexandra had not lost her sense of humor.

"Why don't I cook two of them, and we'll both pretend we're dining out? I'll take you to the Palace Restaurant in New York—it's one of the most expensive."

"That sounds wonderful, Julia. I accept your kind invitation." A wan smile made Alexandra's face light up. "Too bad we don't have some attractive escorts."

Julia thought of Adam. "One should be calling me in a few minutes. He's very attractive.

I'll even let you share him."

Alexandra demanded to hear all about Adam, and the older woman smiled as she watched Julia's animated face describing him to her.

"Do you have three TV dinners, so that I can invite Adam?"

Alexandra began straightening things around her small house.

"Adam won't care how it looks. He used to live only two streets away from here when he was a child."

When the telephone rang, Alexandra agreed that Adam could come for dinner if he wished. He accepted the invitation and Julia was delighted. She went into the kitchen and managed to find a pretty tablecloth, and a small silver vase. Looking out of the back door, she saw a solitary red rose blooming in the desolate back yard. Julia went out and picked it, and brought it back into the little house. Filling the vase with water, she thought of how the rose reminded her of Alexandra. Its beauty lit up the squalid environment. *There was always a touch of God's caring, if we chose to look for it*, she thought.

By the time Adam arrived, Julia had set a small table by the fire in the living room, and as she escorted him in to meet Alexandra the small house began to take on a happier air.

Julia, very quickly, had explained to Adam what had happened to Alexandra, so that he was prepared to meet her. But as he entered the room and saw her, it was obvious that he was shaken. Quickly, he recovered his composure, and went over to be introduced to Alexandra.

Julia noticed that he kept looking at the older woman, an incredulous expression on his face. Turning to Julia, he said, "You won't believe this, but Mrs. Panov reminds me so much of my mother." He turned to Alexandra, and jokingly said, "A few days ago, in New York, I saw someone who reminded me of another person I had known." He looked at Julia and said, "You're going to think that everyone reminds me of someone, but the resemblance to my mother is so striking."

Alexandra said slowly, "What was your last name again?"

"Kingsley."

Alexandra walked over to him, and put her hand on his arm.

"I had a sister who married someone out here in San Francisco. I never met him. She refused to let us know where she was." Searching Adam's eyes, she said, "I seem to remember that her married name *was* Kingsley."

"Was your maiden name Morgan?"

Alexandra answered with a growing sense of anticipation and thrill in her voice, "Yes! My sister's name was Helen . . . . "

Adam said, excitedly, "That *must* have been my mother! She once told me she had a sister, who was a ballet dancer, but that she had lost touch with her." Thinking of his father, who had deserted his family, Adam said, "She was too ashamed to let anyone know about her marriage, until it was too late and she had lost contact with them completely."

Julia watched as Adam leaned down to kiss this woman who had suddenly come into his life. He held her tenderly in his arms, and looking over at Julia—his eyes misting over—he whispered in a low voice, "Thank you for introducing me to my Aunt Alexandra. I feel as if God has given me back my mother . . . "

She felt very strongly that God had brought her out here on one of His special missions, and she felt a warmth in her heart. Thanking Him, she knew that Adam would help to restore Alexandra's feeling of being needed. He had already made Julia feel that her life was not hopeless any more . . . .

Chapter
—10—

That night Julia stayed with Alexandra, but it was decided that the next day she would move to a hotel nearer the heart of San Francisco. Adam had insisted Alexandra stay with him. He was living in the condominium that he had bought for his mother several years before. It seemed only right that Alexandra should make it her home now. What furniture she had would be moved there.

In many ways, it would be easier for Julia as she would be working late most nights, and she found a hotel only a few minutes' walk away from the agency in Union Square.

"I shall feel much happier, knowing you are being taken care of during the day, Alexandra," Julia had told her.

Adam had arranged for a woman to come in and attend to any needs Alexandra might have. The remembrance of Alexandra's expression, when they had eventually persuaded her to stay with Adam, made Julia smile to herself. The worried, hopeless look was gone, and the Alexandra she knew had partly returned. The stroke still left its debilitating marks, but the old spirit was now very apparent.

The agency demanded a great deal of Julia's attention. She understood why Patrick had asked her to come and oversee operations for these weeks. Having only been in the office for a few hours, Julia's innate instinct for organization and public relations had told her that several departments would have to be restructured and re-staffed.

Julia dreaded having to fire anyone—always her heart wanted to overrule any decisions that would involve telling someone they would no longer be required. Bob Coleman, Fraser and Marshall's man in charge, would be given that thankless task, she thought.

This evening Adam was coming to the

agency to take her out to dinner. Julia kept glancing at her watch, eager to see him once again. His boldly handsome face kept emerging in her thoughts and she found herself distracted over and over again.

It was now almost six o'clock, and she still had several key telephone calls to make to the East Coast. She envisioned the office in New York—it would be nine o'clock there and still a hive of frantic activity.

By the time Adam arrived, Julia had finished all her phone calls and was more than ready to enjoy his company and the City of San Francisco. Her heart leaped with excitement as he came into her office and walked straight up to her, circling her with his strong arms.

"I've missed you so, Julia," he murmured, kissing her hair.

She said, tilting her face up to his, "I've missed you, too, Adam." They stood looking into each other's eyes for a few disturbing seconds, then she broke away—reaching for her handbag. "Do you realize I've been here three days and I've hardly seen anything of this spectacular city?"

"I shall change all that immediately," Adam said, taking her arm and kissing her tenderly on the cheek.

They walked out into the evening air, both

eager to enjoy each other's company in one of the world's most exciting metropolises. Union Square was filled with late night shoppers, mostly tourists bent on carrying off some exotic souvenir of their trip. Several young people entertained the passersby with their spellbinding mime, or by playing classical music on a plaintive violin or soulful trumpet.

At the corner of Stockton Street, Adam bought Julia a bunch of miniature violets from the owner of a brightly colored, flower filled cart. The display lit up the gray winter evening.

Julia put the delicately scented flowers up to her nose and took a deep breath. "Mm, they smell like the woods after the rain...how beautiful. Thank you, Adam."

"They're just a reminder of the difference between New York and San Francisco. Right now, on the street corners of New York they're selling roasted chestnuts, and people are desperately banging their hands together trying to keep warm." They laughed together.

Adam put his hand under Julia's elbow and guided her to a cable car that would take them up to Nob Hill. The old car rattled and shook as it ascended, bells rang and people smiled at one another—some hiding the concern of

whether the cable could possibly bear the
weight. Adam held Julia close to him as they
stood among the tightly packed passengers.
His nearness made her pulse leap.

The cable car arrived at Nob Hill, and as Julia
alighted she looked around in amazement.

"How beautiful! Such interesting architec-
ture everywhere. What cathedral is that?" she
asked, pointing to the vast, gothic building
ahead of her. Floodlights made the magnificent structure seem to emerge through the
mist in an almost unreal, supernatural way.

"Oh, that's Grace Cathedral. It's Episcopal,
and just as magnificent inside. I'll have to take
you there one day."

"I'm a great lover of stained glass windows,
and I imagine there are some really glorious
examples," Julia said excitedly.

Crossing the street to the Fairmont Hotel,
she remembered she had read an illustration,
years before, about a stained glass window.

"I recall reading an article that said that a
stained glass window, viewed from the outside doesn't begin to show its beauty. It is only
when it is seen from the inside, with the light
bringing the vibrant colors to life, that the
true beauty can be seen."

Julia looked quickly at Adam. "That it
parallels what happens in our own lives when

Jesus Christ comes in."

Adam nodded his head as they reached the top of the steps leading into the Fairmont. Pausing for a few seconds, before helping Julia through the revolving doors, he said, "It's His light breaking through the darkness that makes us see all the beauty we've missed before."

They smiled at one another, and in the middle of the busy lobby, Adam kissed Julia on the cheek. "I thank Him for the beauty of your life, Julia, and what it means to me...."

"I'm so thankful for you, Adam. We met at just the right time...we both needed to forget, and start to live again."

They had come to a standstill, unaware of the people milling around them. Holding both of each other's hands, they looked affectionately at one another.

It was Adam who became conscious of their surroundings, and ushered Julia into the hotel's Squire Restaurant. Decorated in the elegant victorian manner of early San Francisco, it instantly made Julia relax.

"This is perfect after a very wearying day at the agency." She looked at Adam, thinking, *Perfect because you have the gift of helping me to forget, so often...*

She sensed that Adam was conscious of her

innermost feelings. They were seated at a quiet, inviting table, crisply covered in white linen. Each of them studied their menus. Julia found she was reading about the same dish over and over again—her mind still on Adam, and what he was so quickly beginning to mean to her.

She had seen such a tender side to him, when he had met Alexandra and realized that she was his aunt. His concern for her, and now his day-by-day caring, brought a sudden tear to Julia's eyes.

That first sight of Alexandra had devastated Julia as well as Adam. How terrible to grow older and not have anyone care about you. A shudder went through her, thinking of the loneliness Alexandra must have experienced.

"You look so sad, Julia," Adam said, leaning forward and taking her hand.

She gave a sigh. "I was just thinking about Alexandra, and all she has suffered. It's really wonderful that you two have found each other. To know she has a relative has made all the difference to her life."

"It has to mine. My brother Tom and I still can't quite believe we have found Alexandra who grew up with our mother. It's such a heartwarming feeling—a link with Mother. How I wish you could have met her." Adam's face lit up, remembering the woman who had raised him under such difficult circumstances.

"In many ways I see the same resolute characteristics in Alexandra." Adam continued thoughtfully, "Yesterday, when I came home she was sitting by the window, looking out over the Bay. When she heard my voice she turned and said, 'Adam, how good to know you're home.' Her profile in the twilight and the timbre of her voice made me think for a few seconds that it was my mother."

After they had ordered their meal, Julia said, thoughtfully, "Years ago, when she lived in Bronxville, I would often admire her victorian sewing table. It was placed near a large, bay window by her armchair. While we had tea she would show me the treasures stored inside it. Miniatures of ivory, sewing appliances from the past, pin cushions elaborately embroidered. All had been in her family for years. Each item in the sewing table was exquisite."

Julia relaxed in her chair, smiling as she remembered the warmth and understanding she had always received from Alexandra.

"Well, yesterday, as I was helping to arrange the few pieces of furniture she had managed to save—and which *you* so thoughtfully had delivered from the little house we found her in—I recognized the old sewing table. Alexandra saw me go over to it and run my hands over the graceful lines. She said, 'Julia, I've left that for you in my will. I remember how much you loved it. Each time I have used it I have always thought of you, and prayed for you.' Tears rolled down her cheeks, and with great difficulty, she whispered, 'They were such happy days, weren't they?' "

Julia could not continue, and she felt Adam's hand on hers. So much had happened in all their lives. When she used to visit Alexandra, Neal was still alive and the promise of the future with him had made Julia feel as if life would always hold bright tomorrows. Julia clasped Adam's hand tightly. This friendship had given her new hope—but the memory of days past sent a chill through her . . .

"Julia, our conversation has taken on such a somber note. We should be celebrating— there is so much for which to be thankful."

"You're absolutely right, Adam. I am far too introspective. Forgive me."

Their conversation turned to lighthearted happenings and plans for tomorrow, when Julia would be visiting the Silicon Valley where Adam's factory was situated. It would be helpful for her to see him in action against the background of the revolutionary computer he had designed. Plans for the advertising were going exceedingly well, and she hoped they would be launched at the beginning of December.

"In time for Christmas buying, too," she had told Adam, as the computer was not only designed for the office but could be used very successfully in the home.

Julia felt herself begin to relax again. She felt so fortunate to be with Adam, in such gracious surroundings. Tonight she wanted to forget New York, her work, her past. It was important to her that she try to shed the memories that held her back from living again...

During their first course—both had chosen a gourmet dish recommended by the chef, filet de boeuf in a light, subtle sauce—Adam told her of the different places he had selected to take her. Sausalito, across the Bay, a trip to Monterey, Golden Gate Park—with over a thousand acres of lovely drives, lakes, and gardens, and tea at the Japanese Tea Garden—Chinatown...Adam named so many, Julia laughed with anticipation.

"I shall have to stay twice as long as I had planned to see everything!"

"Precisely my intentions," Adam said

firmly. "I am not about to let you go back to New York..."

His voice trailed off as a group of people entered the dining room. Julia saw his eyes cloud over. His whole countenance changed. She saw him watching a tall young woman, dressed stylishly in what must be a pale blue designer dress. She was blonde, statuesque, and many of the male diners were looking at her walk behind the maitre d' to be seated with her party.

Julia suddenly felt that the charcoal gray suit she was wearing must seem very dull to Adam, even though the white satin blouse contrasted dramatically. She had brushed her hair into a French knot, securing it with a gold, ornate comb. Adam had remarked how glamorous she looked, but now, seeing him watch this vivacious young blonde woman, seated three tables away, Julia felt dowdy, unsure of herself.

Adam resumed eating, but it was clear he was shaken by the presence of the young woman. Julia sensed that their evening had been ruined. Her heart began to beat erratically.

"It's Georgina, isn't it?" Julia asked, her throat constricting.

Adam looked across at her, astounded

by her intuitiveness.

"How did you know?"

"By your reaction. You look as if you have been hit with a sledge hammer." Julia was only saying what she felt, too. Her world with Adam appeared to be caving in.

Georgina was animatedly talking to a distinguished man, many years her senior and seated at her right. His eyes had not left her since entering the restaurant. Julia noticed that Georgina's smile seemed forced, as she turned to include the rest of her party in the conversation.

It was then that Georgina saw Adam. The surprised look on her face was immediately noticed by the older man, and he turned to look in Adam's direction. Julia saw him try to restrain Georgina, who had jumped to her feet. But she shook off his hand, and began walking toward Adam.

Julia felt her mouth go dry . . . she wanted to leave the table before Georgina reached them, but Adam's hand on her arm prevented her . . .

Chapter —11—

"**A**dam!" Georgina approached the table, both hands outstretched. "Oh, Adam, darling, I'm so glad to see you. I've tried calling you . . ."

Georgina's husky, enticing voice grated on Julia. Adam got to his feet and hastily introduced her, but Georgina barely acknowledged her presence.

"*Where* have you been, Adam?" Georgina put her hand on his shoulder; her fingers touched the collar of his suit, drifting down to his lapel. She straightened the handkerchief in his breast pocket, in a familiar, protective way—very conscious that Julia was watching her.

"I've been in New York. When did you get back from France?" Adam's voice sounded hesitant, as if wishing the conversation would end.

"Just a few days ago. I have to see you, Adam. It's very important." Georgina had now turned her back on Julia, and was speaking in a low, confidential tone.

"I'm very busy, Georgina."

"But surely you can find time to talk to me." She now seemed highly nervous and insistent.

"All right. I'll call you tomorrow morning."

Assured that he would, Georgina returned to her table, ignoring Julia, who was by now feeling very uncomfortable.

Adam sat down again and a few moments elapsed. Then he said, "I'm sorry about that, Julia. She completely took me off guard. I had no idea she was back from Europe."

Julia managed a smile. "Well, life is full of surprises. I'm not sure who was more surprised by seeing her—you or me." She thoughtfully continued, "She does resemble the girl you saw in the restaurant in New York. That's how I guessed it was Georgina."

"Oh, yes. I had forgotten that." Changing

the subject, Adam asked, "Would you care for dessert?"

But Julia's appetite had vanished as soon as Georgina had come to their table, and she shook her head. "Perhaps we ought to go, Adam. It is getting rather late."

He signaled for the waiter, and Julia excused herself to go to the powder room. Thankfully it was deserted, and she sat down in front of one of the ornate gold mirrors. Powdering her nose, she studied her face. The expression in her eyes betrayed her. For a while she had felt assured again. Adam had swept into her life, helping to dull the pain that had been her companion for so long. The days spent with him had made her feel alive again. There had actually been hours when she had forgotten Neal.

A painful longing swept over her. Just to be able to run into his arms again—to know he was alive. . .

Julia felt as if she were about to break down, when the sound of the door opening and the voices of two women entering made her steel herself. A quick look in the mirror assured her that Adam would not see how deeply she had been affected by Georgina's sudden appearance.

Adam was waiting for her in the lobby, but

instead of walking with her to the revolving doors, he took her arm and walked to the elevator.

"This won't take long, but I want you to see the view from the roof. That's if it isn't too foggy tonight."

The elevator was crowded with other visitors, but most got off before reaching the rooftop. Adam escorted Julia out into the garden, and there she saw the twinkling, breathtaking lights of San Francisco. It was not a completely clear night, but she was able to distinguish many of the landmarks.

"I love your city, Adam. I think I'm going to agree with Rudyard Kipling when he said, 'San Francisco has only one drawback . . .' tis hard to leave.' " Julia's voice trembled, revealing the emotions she was feeling.

"I'm glad you're not leaving for awhile, Julia. We have many days ahead together . . . "

Adam took her hand and walked with her across the roof to the other side. They watched the cars driving down Nob Hill, conscious of the nearness of each other.

There was so much Julia wanted to say to Adam, but she could not bring herself to begin —she knew she could so easily break down. Georgina had completely devastated the secure emotions Julia had been experiencing.

From the roof of the hotel the cathedral loomed up before her. It gave her an assurance of permanence. Why couldn't she accept the fact that whatever happened she could be confident of God's love for her? Again, the turmoil she had felt for so long welled up inside of her.

Adam had been silent—watching the brilliant scene. "Julia, just because we saw Georgina tonight doesn't mean that anything has changed. I hope you realize that . . . she had begun to feel less important to me. Seeing her was rather disconcerting. When you've known someone as long as I've known Georgina, she becomes part of your life. A habit that needs to be broken . . ."

"I know. I understand." Julia did not want to talk about it. She knew it would be easy to love this man, and if there were any chance that Georgina was wanting Adam to forgive her and return to their former relationship, then Julia wanted to protect herself.

"Thank you for showing me the view, Adam."

He swung her around to him, and before she knew what was happening he had taken her into the circle of his arms. His physical strength made her feel breathless, and his nearness made her forget all her resolutions about wanting to protect herself from being hurt.

"Julia, you've come to mean so much to me." Adam's eyes traveled over her face, and her feelings for him intensified. "I've been hurt by Georgina. I never thought I could trust another woman, and then you came into my life, Julia."

His cheek against hers felt so persuasive—causing her to want to tell him what he had come to mean to her. But she remained silent, even though her heart was beating wildly.

An almost inaudible, "Oh, Adam..." escaped her.

Julia was hardly aware how long they were standing there, locked in each other's arms. She was only conscious of the heaving of Adam's chest, crushed against her and the deep, exciting kisses that transported her beyond reality.

Another couple walked by them, and Julia pulled away from Adam.

"We really must go," she whispered.

Adam kissed her gently on the curve of her lips. "I know, but I don't want to, Julia."

Slowly, they walked toward the elevator. Even though these moments with Adam had been so intensely, passionately theirs, Julia wished that her heart did not ache so, that she did not have a sense of foreboding about Georgina...

• • •

Adam was late picking Julia up at her hotel the next morning. He apologized several times, but Julia said she understood.

Later, as they drove toward his factory in the Silicon Valley, he hesitatingly told her that Georgina had not wanted him to end their telephone conversation.

"It was a very tearful Georgina that I spoke with this morning."

Julia looked out of the window, not offering to ask why.

Adam continued, "She told me she had made a mistake, that the man who was with her last night was the one whom she had thought she was in love with in France. Seeing him here, in a setting familiar to her, she realized it had been a big mistake."

Julia said quietly, "She's still in love with you?"

"Yes, and she wants us to marry." Adam was at a loss to know what else to say—Julia too shaken to answer.

They arrived at the factory, and she was grateful for the diversion. It was an impressive complex and she was amazed at what Adam had accomplished in such a short time. He deserved to achieve—the hard work that had gone into this project was apparent everywhere she looked. Adam showed her through the factory. The assembly lines, packaging departments, shipping, all were on the grand tour. Finally, they arrived at the suite of offices.

Adam introduced Julia to his secretary, then took Julia into his private office and closed the door.

"Well, what do you think of it all?"

"You've accomplished so much. I'm really impressed. I want our advertising to do your product justice."

Adam stepped closer to Julia and took her hand. "Thank you, I know it will, with you in charge."

Their conversation was shadowed by the realization of Georgina's return and change of heart. Both knew that this had cast a pall over their relationship.

Adam's telephone rang, and it was evident to Julia who was calling. A weariness came over Adam's face.

"I really can't talk to you now . . . I'm very busy." He put down the telephone, after assuring the caller he would call back later. Letting out a long sigh, he said, "I never dreamed Georgina would change her mind."

"A woman's preogative," Julia said lightly, hiding how she really felt. She knew she must face this objectively. "I don't blame her. You are much more attractive than her escort of last night!"

Her seeming lightheartedness caused Adam to laugh, and the mood was changed. Plans were for him to take Julia to meet his brother Tom, at his church on the Peninsula, have dinner and then attend an evening service. Julia had been looking forward to meeting Tom. Adam had spoken so highly of him, and she wanted to meet some of the young people who had been helped by the drug rehabilitation program at the church.

I've got to stop being so introspective, Lord. There are so many who need to know they are loved by You.

• • •

Tom's church in San Mateo was still in the growing stages. A mission church, only started a year ago, it had attracted many who needed to find answers to their lives—especially young drug addicts. The bright, white wooden structure had been built by several

of the church members, and Julia felt welcome
as soon as she stepped through the main
doors.

Adam waved to Tom, who was talking to
the young organist. He came up to them and
the warmth of his smile made Julia immediately feel at home.

"Julia, I've heard so much about you from
Adam. Yes, you didn't exaggerate one bit,"
Tom said, looking at his younger brother. "It
used to be quite a fault of his, but then a lot
has changed in your life, hasn't it, Adam?"

A good natured punch from Adam hushed
him. "You don't have to tell Julia all my faults
as soon as you meet her. This, believe it or not,
is my ministerial brother. I still say you looked
the least likely candidate on graduation day
at the seminary."

Tom's relaxed personality, the shock of
blonde hair—reminiscent of his brother's—
and his unconventional clothes, made Julia see
he would be a natural for reaching young people with their problems.

Dinner was "potluck" in the church hall,
and Julia was introduced to several of the
young members who, only a few months before, had been rescued from the vicious hold
of debilitating drugs. While she talked with
them, she noticed a girl who never seemed

quite at ease and who hung back from the rest
of the crowd.

Her face had a sad, furtive expression. Julia
felt drawn to her. She could see in her eyes
a sadness that could not be disguised by any
of the heavy makeup. The long, straggly
brown hair hid part of her face, almost as if
she wanted to conceal the hurt and hopelessness that she felt.

"Hello, my name is Julia Marshall. I'm new
here, too." Julia put out her hand to the young
woman, and after a few moments hesitation
she responded.

"Oh...yes...hello..." the girl seemed at
a loss for words.

"What's your name," Julia asked kindly.

"Rebecca..."

"It's a beautiful name. Do you live near
here?"

The girl thought for a few seconds. "Well,
I hope to. I just arrived, as it were. I've been
living in San Francisco, but some friends said
it was easier out here to find a place to stay
on a permanent basis."

"I imagine it would be. I'm from New York
—just here for a few weeks. I'd like to be able
to help you, if I could. Do you have a job?"

Rebecca hesitated. "Not really. I haven't been
able to keep a job. My...health, you know."

"I'm sure the church has somewhere you could stay." Julia saw the girl clench her fist— fighting any thought of being entangled with the church.

"Oh, it's not a place where they would expect you to join, or anything like that. Just somewhere for you to be able to live until you were feeling better."

Rebecca said slowly, "I'd like that. I need a place to sleep and forget..." Tears had formed and she brushed them away with a defiant gesture. "I don't need any charity. I'm fine really. Just a little tired."

Adam joined them and Julia introduced him to Rebecca. He asked her if she would be staying for the service, as he would like her to sit with them.

Dazedly, Rebecca looked around the room, trying to comprehend why people were being nice to her. "O.K. I don't see any harm," she said, a little defiantly.

The service was geared for young people, and Julia found herself thinking how different the services were at her church in New York. But the message, basically, was the same. One of love and forgiveness, and a hope for tomorrow in Jesus Christ. Tom's easy style spoke directly to those who were gathered there. His concern and love for them and his utter lack of personal condemnation had a deep effect.

"We all need forgiveness in our lives," his resonant, understanding voice rang out through the small church. "Jesus Christ came that we could know forgiveness. It's not enough to just believe in Him—He wants you to know Him personally. Do you? Or have you just known about Him all your life. There's a difference. And it isn't until you know Him as Lord and Savior that you begin to live as He planned for you to live—spiritually alive, knowing what real happiness is. Not the euphoric high that comes from drugs and fades, but a joy that is lasting."

Julia noticed that Rebecca, who was sitting next to her, was shifting uncomfortably in the pew. Her straggly hair completely hid her face from Julia, but she sensed that Rebecca was crying. Julia put her hand out to her and she clutched it—her long nails digging into Julia.

After the service was over, Rebecca remained seated, leaning forward in the pew—her head still bowed.

"Rebecca, can I help you?" Julia asked quietly.

"I don't think so," came the unexpected answer. "It's all too late for that."

"Why do you think it's too late?"

Rebecca continued to look down at the floor.

"I've tried all this before. It doesn't work, you know."

"Perhaps you didn't give our Lord a chance. Were you expecting quick, easy solutions to something that has become such an addiction?"

Julia had noticed needle marks on Rebecca's arms. She had gone beyond marijuana to the ruthless addiction of heroin.

"It's the daily knowledge that He loves you, Rebecca, that His strength and courage are there that can help you overcome anything."

Rebecca looked up at Julia, her expression one of belligerence. "What if I mess up? What if I fail?"

"Then you pick yourself up, and realize that He still loves you and forgives you. It's like a baby learning to walk. It's hard work, but with determination you will succeed, Rebecca."

Julia could see that the girl was deep in thought. Surprisingly, Rebecca said, "Would you have lunch with me one day in San Francisco? We could have a sandwich in the park, or something."

"I'd like that, Rebecca. How about Friday in Union Square?"

The young girl smiled. "O.K. About noon?"

Julia nodded. "Fine. I'm working at an

agency right on the Square. I'll bring the sandwiches. But first, I'll find out if you can stay at the rehab center for a few days."

She took Rebecca over to Tom, who welcomed her and said she could stay as long as she liked. After being assured Rebecca had enough money for her fare into San Francisco, Julia hugged her and said she would be looking forward to Friday.

Adam had watched Julia as she had talked with Rebecca. When they left the church, he said, "You are a natural counselor, Julia, I saw a different expression on that girl's face after she finished talking with you."

"It helps me, too, Adam. As I was talking to her I kept thinking about my own life. I have expected God to instantly take away my grief. But it's when we reach out and try to help others that the healing begins. . ."

Adam took her hand and they walked out of the church. Julia was glad they had come there—in her heart she felt strengthened.

During the service she had prayed that God would help her in the days ahead, for so much seemed to be going on in Adam's life now. She had felt an important part of it, but with Georgina perhaps back in his life Julia knew she might have to prepare herself to say "good bye" to him. . . .

Chapter
—*12*—

Friday, noon, Union Square was beginning to fill with office workers on their lunch hour. Julia walked through it—armed with sandwiches for her lunch with Rebecca. She found a bench and sat down, watching for the girl who had so touched her heart. She prayed that she would be able to help her; at the same time wondering whether Rebecca might have changed her mind about meeting her today.

Julia's eyes strayed to the tall buildings surrounding the square. She saw a man lean out of one of the windows and wave to a girl, who was laughing up at him.

Julia remembered a day in Central Park, when she had gone for a walk by herself. Neal had been working on a deadline, and she had decided to leave him in the apartment while she went to get some air. Whenever she had done this, she would often look up to the tenth floor at their apartment, thinking of him there and a warm feeling of love would surge through her. On this particular day she looked up and had seen him watching her. Then she saw he was signaling SOS with a flashlight. Over and over she saw the signal, and began to run back toward Fifth Avenue. Her heart had been beating so loudly, she thought everyone she passed would have heard it. The traffic light had seemed to take forever to change. When it did, she raced ahead of all the other people—up Fifth Avenue to their apartment building, through the lobby, up in the elevator and finally—out of breath—she had burst into their apartment.

"What's the matter, Neal?" she had cried.

Neal had come strolling out of the living room, and very calmly had said, "I couldn't stand to be without you for another moment." He had then taken her in his arms and kissed her passionately.

Julia had wanted to be angry with him, but

he completely disarmed her. She remembered
the look on his face. His eyes had burned with
such love for her. They had walked back into
the living room and he had held her in his
arms, whispering, "I never want to be apart
from you, Julia..."

Remembering the incident as she sat in the
Square, tears gathered in Julia's eyes. She was
completely unaware of her surroundings until
a "Hi" brought her back to the present.

Standing before her was Rebecca, looking
concerned at seeing Julia's tears.

"Are you all right?" she asked, futilely
pushing back the hair from her face.

Startled, Julia apologized for not having seen
her. A pain still lingered around her heart and
she quickly wiped away her tears.

"I'm so glad to see you, Rebecca. I wondered
if you would be able to come."

"There's nothing on my agenda right now,"
Rebecca said with a smile. "I've cleared my
social calendar, and here I am."

Julia offered her a sandwich and a can of
cola, and together they began to eat their
lunch—amid the crowds who had now gathered. The sun was shining hazily through the
clouds, making the mood of the crowd almost
festive. Rebecca noticed some of the younger
people who were obviously on drugs. Julia

saw her watching them intently.

Rebecca said, "You know, I thought an awful lot about what you said the other night, and what I heard in the church. I don't want to waste my life anymore, Julia. Do you think God would give me a second chance?"

"Of course He will. He goes on loving us and forgiving our foolishness. He's forgiven me over and over again." Julia looked directly at Rebecca and said, quietly, "Do you really mean that you want to give your life to Jesus Christ?" The girl nodded. "You want His forgiveness for the past?" Again Rebecca nodded, only this time more emphatically.

"Why don't you pray, Rebecca, and ask Jesus to forgive the past and come into your life."

"Yes," Rebecca said quietly, her eyes filling with tears, "I'd like that."

Julia took her hand and very softly Rebecca began to pray, "Dear Lord Jesus, thank You for dying for me—forgive my sins and come into my life that I now give over to You."

Julia put her arms around her shoulders and hugged her. "I feel so happy for you, Rebecca. You'll see, your life will really begin to mean something now. Don't ever forget how much you are loved by God, will you?"

"I won't," she said, a smile now appearing on her cherubic face.

Julia noticed that Rebecca had a large box of cereal with her and wondered if she had brought it in case Julia had forgotten to bring the sandwiches. As she was staring at it, Rebecca suddenly handed it to her.

"I want you to have this. I've got my needles and heroin in there. I want you to see I mean business."

Julia, who had been leaning against the back of the bench, now sat up straight—alarmed, but not wanting to let Rebecca see.

"And what am I supposed to do with it?"

"Throw it away. Then I won't be tempted."

Thoughts of the illegality of possession flashed through Julia's mind, but she did not want to discourage Rebecca.

"I feel better now," Rebecca said, seeing the box in Julia's hands. Julia wished she did.

"It's like starting to live all over again," the young girl said as if an enormous burden had been taken from her.

Julia put the box under the seat and sat hiding it with her legs—thankful for Rebecca's determination to overcome her habit, but concerned about the drug paraphernalia in the innocent looking box. Its dispoal was top priority.

Realizing that Rebecca could never hope to find a job looking the way she did, Julia said,

"I'd like to take you to one of the stores and buy you a dress, if you wouldn't mind."

The girl looked down at her grubby jeans, and smiled. "You don't think these are fancy enough?"

"Well, I want to introduce you to someone this afternoon who very probably might hire you. I'd like you to make a good impression."

"If it means getting a job, I'll gladly accept your offer of a dress, because that means I'll be able to pay you back."

"Great," Julia said, jumping up—then she realized the cereal box was still under the bench. Hastily she picked it up and shoved it into her tote bag. Trying not to walk too suspiciously, she ushered Rebecca out of Union Square, into Macy's Department Store and walked straight to the ladies' room. The heroin was flushed down the toilet, and Julia squashed the box tightly around the syringes and dumped it into a waste can.

Grabbing Rebecca's hand, she whisked her into the junior department and with a sigh of relief she proceeded to help her choose a dress. This led to handbag, shoes, stockings, underwear, and a raincoat.

They went into a ladies room on another floor—Julia could not face going back to the same one—and Rebecca changed into her new outfit. Julia brushed her hair up off of her face, securing it with one of her own combs.

"I never knew how very pretty you were, Rebecca. I was only able to see half of your face before!"

Rebecca smiled and her whole face lit up as she looked in the mirror and saw her new image. "I bet I get that job looking like this!"

Julia laughed. "I bet you do too, Rebecca!"

She walked back with her to the agency and asking Rebecca to sit in the waiting room, went in search of Bob Coleman and quickly told him about Rebecca.

"We need a girl to take care of all the odd jobs here, Bob. She's very bright and needs a break right now in her life."

Bob Coleman smiled ingratiatingly at Julia. "I've heard that your mother is one of the leading charity organizers in New York . . ."

Julia turned on him and said, spiritedly, "This is not charity, Bob. She's a girl who is talented and just needs someone to believe in her. Please see she is taken care of—all right?"

Bob Coleman saw the determined look in Julia's eyes, and hurriedly assured her that he would personally see Rebecca was treated well.

After Rebecca found out she had been hired at Fraser and Marshall's, she hugged Julia. "You must have quite a lot of influence here. Thanks a lot!"

Around 3 P.M. Julia left the office. She wanted to visit Alexandra before Adam came back from the factory. Thinking over all that had happened, Julia had felt she should try to stay out of Adam's way for a few days, giving him time to resolve the question of Georgina.

Julia missed him terribly. The days seemed empty. A talk with Alexandra was just what she needed, and as she rang the bell of Adam's condominium she prayed that she would have the strength to carry out the promise she had made to herself not to see him.

Alexandra opened the door, looking almost like she used to in New York. Her hair was groomed, and there was a radiant smile on her face. A soft beige, lace dress, with a long strand of pearls caught at the neck with one of her antique brooches, made Alexandra look like the prima ballerina she once was.

"You look wonderful, Alexandra!" Julia exclaimed, kissing her. "I do believe you'll be dancing Swan Lake again!"

"Hardly, my dear Julia," Alexandra laughed, still having to rely on her elegant cane. "But I feel so much better—who knows!"

She led Julia into the living room, which overlooked the Bay. The great expanse of sea shone in the sunlight, and Julia picked out the

different well known landmarks—the Golden
Gate Bridge, San Quentin, Sausalito across the
Bay. Scores of brightly colored boats added to
the brilliance of the scene.

"What a fantastic view, Alexandra. I know
you must be happy here."

"I am, Julia, I am. Adam has been so kind.
He's made me feel that this is my home now.
God has really blessed me."

A tray had been set on a table by the window and Julia quickly made them some tea.

"It's just like the Bronxville days, Alexandra. How I loved coming to visit you. I always
left with such good advice—feeling as if I could
accomplish anything."

Alexandra searched Julia's face. "Why is it
I sense you want my advice today?"

Julia took a deep breath and walked over to
the window, her back to Alexandra. "I never
could fool you, could I?"

"No. I know you too well, Julia. You want
that expression on your face to tell the world
everything is fine, but deep down I know
something is troubling you, child."

"I made up my mind, as I rang the door bell
today—I would not cry—I would not get into
any of my problems—and now here we are
. . . I haven't even had my tea . . ."

Julia ran and knelt down by Alexandra and

the older woman put her arms around her. "Tell me what is troubling you, Julia."

Julia hardly knew where to start. "I'm so confused. I still grieve for Neal, yet I think I am falling in love with Adam. I believe he cares for me..." Alexandra began to say something. "No, please, don't say anything until I tell you everything. Has Adam told you about Georgina?"

Alexandra nodded. Julia continued, "Well, you know she wants him back. I don't feel right about my feelings for him, if that is what they both want..."

Waiting for the torrent of words to end, Alexandra watched Julia's beautiful face—the questioning in her enormous brown eyes, the long, black lashes fringed with unshed tears.

"What do you think God wants for you and Adam?" Alexandra asked gently.

"I don't know. I had tried to pray about it, but I don't seem to get anywhere... part of me still feels guilty even thinking about loving another man. I don't even know if I could make Adam happy. Would the memory of Neal always come between us?" Julia looked up at Alexandra inquiringly.

"Don't you think that Neal would want you to have someone to take care of you, to love you? Would he have wanted you to be alone for the rest of your life? I remember how he always wanted you to be happy, Julia. His first thoughts were always of you—of what you would want—what you would like."

Julia, fighting back the tears, whispered, "I know, I know. But even if I could love Adam as he deserves to be loved, I can't stand in the way of his love for Georgina."

"How do you know he still loves her?" Alexandra asked firmly. "Are you taking it for granted that he does?"

"He adores her, Alexandra. When we first met he told me he was still getting over the hurt of her rejecting him."

"I think seeing her the other night at the restaurant made him realize that he had changed so much since giving his life to the Lord—and meeting you."

Julia looked at Alexandra, searching the gray-blue eyes that were reminiscent of Adam's. "He told you that?"

"Yes. Over breakfast this morning. I know he's fighting the emotions he once felt for Georgina—she's deliberately playing on them. Adam is like a huge teddy bear, with a heart far too big for his own good. He loves *you*, Julia."

"He told you. . .?"

"Yes, but he didn't even have to—it's there

in his eyes, in his voice each time he mentions your name."

A smile came over Julia's face. "He's such a wonderful person, Alexandra." She brushed the tears from her eyes and got to her feet. "I don't want to be here when he comes back. I just wanted to see you, and ask you to pray for me—us—all three of us, Alexandra."

Alexandra smiled that knowing smile of hers. "And what do you think I've been doing while sitting here, watching this incredible view?"

"Thank you, dear Alexandra. I love you." Julia kissed her on the cheek and walked over to where she had left her handbag and raincoat.

"I must go. I'll call you very soon. God bless."

Julia indicated for Alexandra to remain seated. "I'll see myself out," and walked to the door, just as a key was being put into the lock from outside.

The door opened and there stood Adam, a surprised look on his face . . .

"Julia! How great to see you. You're not leaving are you?"

The sight of Adam standing there, his blonde hair slightly ruffled and a smudge of dark shadows beneath his eyes, made Julia forget the promise she had made to herself about not seeing him for a few days.

"I insist we have dinner, Julia. Let's go over to Sausalito on the ferry and see the skyline of San Francisco from there...you'll love it..."

Julia found herself agreeing...

Chapter
—13—

The ferry ride across the Bay was glorious. Julia leaned over the railing, watching the skyline of San Francisco move farther and farther away, but was more conscious of Adam's arm around her shoulder and the joy she felt in his presence.

Once they docked at Sausalito, a few minutes' walk brought them to a picturesque restaurant that seemed to cling to the side of the wooded hills, which swept down to the sea.

The evening was warm enough for them to

sit outside under one of the pink umbrellas for which the charming restaurant was well known. Julia looked back over the Bay toward the brilliant skyline . . .

"What a spectacular view!" she said, breathlessly. "I'm trying to remember every detail, so I can visualize it on a rainy day in New York."

Adam watched Julia—the sea breeze gently caressed her long, luxuriant hair. Her tapered fingers pushed the stray tendrils back from her arrestingly lovely eyes.

"I don't want to even think of you returning to New York, Julia."

She turned to look at him, knowing what she had to say would not be welcomed. "I'm going back earlier than planned, Adam. The changes at the agency have gone much more smoothly than we all anticipated." Julia saw a look of dejection in his eyes. She turned away. "I'd like to be home for Thanksgiving. Mother would be very disappointed if I were not there . . ."

"Alexandra will be very disappointed, too. She had planned for us all to dine together. In fact, when I left this morning she said she was going to write a list of all the things we would need—she was going to supervise the whole meal."

"I'm sorry, Adam, I should get back . . ."

"Are you running away, Julia?" Adam's voice bored deep inside her.

She had always been truthful with him—she could not hide her true feelings now. "Perhaps you're right, I am, in a sense, running away. But I want you to really be able to work out your feelings for Georgina."

"What about you, Julia? Are you just being noble, or are you afraid to face how we might feel about each other—we two . . . ?"

Adam leaned forward in his seat, cupping her chin in his hand. "Don't you think that we have a future together?"

She laced her fingers together, looking down at her wedding ring, glistening in the candlelight.

"I can't shut out the memories, Adam." She faltered, finding it hard to go on. Then, "Today in Union Square I remembered an incident that made me return so vividly to my apartment in New York . . . and Neal."

Julia told Adam about Neal signaling from their apartment window, and how desperate she had felt running back there.

"The culmination of that incident was that the police arrived, having seen Neal's urgent SOS from across the park. When we told them what had happened they were not amused!"

She found herself laughing at the memory of the burly police sergeant lecturing them about practical jokes and wasting his time.

Adam laughed with her, then he became serious once more. "We can't erase our memories, Julia. They will fade, but don't try to put them aside. Remember the happy ones and be thankful for all you had." He saw her eyes cloud over and tenderly took her hand. "I know it still hurts, but as Christians we don't grieve hopelessly. You'll see Neal again one day. Don't you believe that?"

"Yes, I do. But I have to resolve all this on my own, Adam. I keep wondering, too, if I will always be looking over my shoulder expecting Georgina to arrive on the scene—or in your memory. I don't want to spend the rest of my life being jealous of memories."

Julia put her hand up to her forehead, brushing back her hair and wishing she had not been so transparent.

Adam smiled. "Julia, I know this—I have fallen in love with you during these last few weeks. Georgina is only someone from my past as far as I am concerned. Of course, there will be memories at times, but they won't be important to me because now I see her in a very different light. Besides, loving someone does not give one the right to own them one hundred percent. I can't forbid you to ever think of Neal, can I?"

He was so earnest and gentle, yet so strong. Julia felt as if she wanted to get up from her chair and put her arms around him. He looked so troubled, like a small boy who could not understand the big world around him. But Julia held back. . . . Still deep within her was the numb, barren feeling she had experienced ever since Neal's death.

"No, I don't suppose anyone has the right to own a person. But you deserve to be loved completely, Adam, and I still find myself holding on to the past."

"Don't do that forever, Julia. You could miss great happiness now."

"I know," she said sadly, "I really do know that. Perhaps I need more time, Adam. . ."

•   •   •

That night, Julia could not sleep. She kept thinking of their conversation in Sausalito. On the ferry ride back to San Francisco, Adam had held her in his arms and whispered, "I love you, Julia. . .with all my heart. Please believe me."

She had wanted to tell him that she loved him too. Now, as she lay in the dark, she was angry with herself. She *was* running away from him. Tomorrow her plane would leave for New York, and there was so much to be resolved.

Julia switched on the bedside lamp. Sleep was elusive and the darkness always made problems seem as if they could never be worked out.

In the loneliness of the hotel room, she began to pray. "Lord, let me love again. I mean really, truly, deep down in my heart. Let me love You again. Take away the emptiness. Show me what holds me back and help me deal with it. . . ."

Her prayer was interrupted by the telephone ringing. Immediately she thought it must be Adam. She glanced at her travel clock and saw it was only 3 A.M. Surely he would not call at such a late hour? But perhaps he too could not sleep.

"Hello?"

"Julia, it's me, Rebecca. I'm scared. I want a fix so badly. I know I can't hold out. . ."

Julia sat up in bed and swung her legs over the side. "Where are you, Rebecca?"

"I'm just down the road from the rehab center."

"Why didn't you tell someone there?"

"I didn't want to disappoint them, Julia.

They all think I'm doing so well." The girl's voice trembled, and Julia could tell she was on the verge of tears.

"Rebecca, it's the most natural thing to happen. They won't judge you. They understand. Some of the counselors have gone through the same experience themselves. You can't expect something so habit-forming, that's been controlling your body for so long, not to try to make you submit again."

"Julia, I feel so close to you—like you understand because you've gone through a lot of pain, too. Please, please, help me..."

Julia prayed she would be able to find the right words to help this desperate girl. "Rebecca, listen to me. You've given your life to Jesus Christ and He promises He will be with you *always*. He loves you and He understands your temptation. Remember Jesus was tempted many times."

There was a moment's silence, and then Julia heard Rebecca weeping. "Why am I so weak, Julia?"

"We are all weak, Rebecca, only some of us have weaknesses that are easily hidden. We can act in front of people as if nothing is wrong, but we cannot hide our frailties from Him. Don't you think I need to trust Him more in my own life, Rebecca?"

"You seem to have it so all together, Julia."

"No I don't, Rebecca. I've learned to conceal many of my faults. There's so much that needs forgiving . . ."

Rebecca's voice sounded relieved. "I thought I was the only one of us that needed forgiveness." Then she said thoughtfully, "Is it because we don't love Jesus enough? When we fail, is it really a lack of love?"

Julia thought how perceptive this young girl was—it was the lack of love for the Lord in her own life that had held her back from finding healing for her memories.

"Yes, Rebecca, it's true. He is always with us. We don't need more of His presence. He needs more of our love. That's what I need to give Him right now."

Julia prayed with Rebecca over the telephone, and then haltingly, Rebecca prayed a sweet, innocent prayer of one who had newly found Jesus' love.

"Thank you, Lord, for loving us. I know you are with us right now. I want to hold on to Your love, so teach me to love You as I should. Bless Julia, she needs to love You more, too. Thank you for letting her be my friend . . ."

When Julia put down the telephone, Rebecca had promised to return to the rehab center. She sounded so much stronger. Julia was grateful that through Rebecca the Lord had been quietly ministering to her. . . .

• • •

The next morning, Julia packed quickly, then made her way up to Nob Hill and the great cathedral. Before she left for New York she wanted to see the stained glass windows, and quietly pray in the peace of that vast edifice.

Julia entered through the enormous doors and walked down the long nave, her footsteps echoing softly. The light shining through the magnificent windows cast radiant patterns. Julia was transfixed by the beauty of it all.

She sat down in the south transept, her eyes never leaving the stained glass window ahead of her.

Adam's voice came back to her—the night he had taken her to the Fairmont Hotel and they had talked about the stained glass windows coming to life when the light shone through them.

"It's His light breaking through our darkness that makes us see all the beauty we've missed before."

The myriad of colors seemed to burst forth from the window ahead of her—vibrant, alive, a burst of praise to the Lord. Julia knelt to pray, tears pouring down her cheeks.

"I want to love You, Lord, as I should. Did I put Neal before You? Did I put him on a pedestal and make You second in my life? I'm so confused. Am I afraid to love again?"

As she knelt there she began to realize that rooted deep down within her was the fear that she could lose Adam. If she gave her heart completely to him, would he be taken from her—just like Neal?

"I want to re-dedicate my life to You, Lord. Like David in the Psalms, 'Restore to me the joy of my salvation.' Lord, restore to me the love I had for You when I gave my life to You..."

The organ had begun to quietly play and Julia realized that people were gathering for a service. She looked at her watch and realized that her plane was leaving in just over two hours.

Tiptoeing out of the cathedral, she saw that it had begun to rain. Her red umbrella protecting her, she walked down the street conscious that God was answering her prayer. There was a peace that had not been there for so long...

●   ●   ●

At the airport, after returning her rental car, Julia hurried to the gate where the plane would be leaving for New York. She approached the airline employee and handed him her ticket. He noted that her seat had already been assigned and told her that she would be boarding in just a few minutes.

Julia walked over to the great plate glass windows and watched as preparations for the flight were taking place. Luggage was being stowed aboard. She felt at peace, but her heart ached for Adam. She had to be sure of her love—and his. She wanted to be sure, too, that their love would always be centered in Jesus Christ.

A touch on her shoulder made Julia spin around. There was Adam and she felt his arms around her.

"You were leaving without saying "Good-bye'?" he asked sadly.

"I don't like 'Good byes,' Adam," Julia whispered, searching the gray-blue eyes she had grown to love. Her heart had begun to beat wildly. "How did you know when my plane was leaving?"

"I phoned the agency." Adam looked down at her, searching her eyes and Julia felt her heart seem to turn over.

"I want you to marry me, Julia. I want you

to give me your answer very soon."

The intensity of their feelings made Julia want to say, "I can give it to you now—it's YES!" but still something held her back.

"Flight number 231 is now boarding for New York."

The impersonal voice interrupted Adam, as he told her, "I need you so much in my life, Julia . . . ."

"Georgina needs you, too, Adam."

"Don't you believe that episode in my life is all over?" Adam took Julia's hand in his and touched her wedding ring. " 'Til death do us part' is what you promised, Julia." The finality of those words seared through her. "Neal would want you to live again."

"I know he would, Adam." Tears were glistening in her eyes. "Just give me a little more time . . ."

There were now only a few passengers waiting to board and Julia kissed Adam quickly on the cheek.

"Au revoir," she whispered, turning to leave.

Adam caught her arm and swung her back to him, kissing her deeply on the lips.

"I'll call you tonight, Julia. Safe trip, darling."

Chapter
—14—

Julia's Manhattan apartment was a welcome sight. The familiar, relaxing atmosphere helped her to shed some of the tensions she had been feeling. The flight from San Francisco had seemed never-ending.

It's so good to be home, she thought glancing around the apartment and taking in the furnishings that had become so much a part of her.

Julia had been handed a mountain of mail by the doorman, and she hastily glanced through it to see if anything might look urgent. A postmark from England caught her eye. She saw by the return address that it was from the ancestry research company, in reply to her inquiry about Adam's possible connection to the family who had owned Kingsley Manor.

Julia walked over to the muted pink sofa and sat down—completely lost in reading about the Kingsley family tree. She remembered the day Adam had visited her family home on Long Island and had been so intrigued by the panelling and mantlepiece that had come from Kingsley Manor in England. She had written the next day to this research company, wanting to surprise Adam with the results.

The ancestry company outlined the Kingsley family tree, noting at the end that because there had been no apparent heir the family had been thought to have died out. However, with the information that Julia had been able to supply, they were now able to verify that Adam and his brother Tom were descendants. The manor house had been sold to pay taxes.

Julia got up from the sofa, and took the letter and its contents to her bedroom. Kicking off her shoes, she lay down on the four-poster bed and continued to trace Adam's heritage. It was exciting to see it all in black and white. He would be so surprised when she gave this to him.

A feeling of longing swept over her, realizing he was three thousand miles away.

Looking up at the ceiling, she thought, *I miss two men now, Lord.* Neal was still very strongly in her mind, but now Adam was equally possessing her thoughts. The memory of their time together in San Francisco brought tears to her eyes. She had begun to feel blissfully happy with him—his kisses had made her body long for his touch.

Georgina's face came into her thoughts—Julia remembered that night when she had come up to Adam while they were dining at the Fairmont. The way Georgina had so possessively touched Adam . . .

Julia got up off the bed, flinging back her hair in an almost defiant gesture. She would unpack and try to put the memory of all that had happened out of her mind.

The telephone rang, and Julia ran toward it—hoping it was Adam.

"Julia! You're home. I've really missed you, dear."

It was her mother. Disappointed at first, Julia sensed a desire to be with her parents. She had grown so independent of them, now she wished she were at the old house on Long Island.

Mrs. Taylor asked about Alexandra and Adam, and Julia told her most of the up-to-date news. She held back telling her mother how she felt about Adam—not even telling of his love for her. Julia concentrated on Alexandra and the happiness she had experienced finding that Adam was her nephew.

"She's not alone anymore, Mother. Adam is like a son to her..."

Julia's voice broke slightly, and her mother sensed that her daughter had so much more to tell her. But now was not the time to press her. Their conversation turned to Rebecca and Julia brightened considerably as she told her mother about the young girl.

"She ended up helping me more than I can say, Mother. She needs our prayers, but I do believe that the Lord has a very wonderful life ahead for her."

"We really should think about how we can help the young people here in New York, Julia. Maybe I could form a committee..."

Julia laughed. "Mother, another committee?"

"Julia, I'm very serious now."

"I know you are, Mother. I'm just teasing you, you know that."

"We are looking forward to Thanksgiving. You will be with us now, won't you?"

"Of course, Mother. I came home early especially so I could be with you and Dad. I'll drive over early Thursday morning and try to avoid the traffic. I'll probably stay right through the weekend."

Mrs. Taylor was delighted. "Don't work too hard until then, Julia. I do worry about you, you know."

"I know, Mother. I'm really tied up with the advertising for Adam's computers, but that should only take me the next couple of days. It will be wonderful to be able to relax with you and Dad. I'm really looking forward to it . . . ."

Julia finished unpacking and got ready for bed. The flight had drained her—unlike the one she had taken with Adam to San Francisco. Their conversation then had made the hours fly by and she had felt exhilarated when they had landed.

"I love you, Julia. . ." Adam's words came back to her as she lay in the solitariness of the great four-poster bed. She was deeply conscious of the vast expanse of smooth white sheet beside her that remained unruffled—as if waiting for Neal or Adam. . .

Neal—Adam.

Adam—Neal.

She sat up in bed. Her hands over her eyes,

trying to blot out the thoughts. But they only seemed to increase. Julia switched on the light by her bed and reached for her Bible. She longed for the peace that she had experienced in the cathedral only that morning.

Out of all the painful, paralyzing memories, Lord, I know I can find Your joy once more.

Julia read a familiar passage—one that she had read often in the past. Martha had told Jesus that if only He had been there, her brother Lazarus would not have died. Julia had thought of these words so often. If only the Lord had spared Neal, how different her life would be.

Then she read the words, "Jesus wept." Familiar words, yet now they seemed to invade her. The consciousness that He shared Julia's sorrow brought tears to her eyes.

Lord Jesus, take the "if onlys" out of my life. I can accept the past and hand it all over to You. I still can't understand everything that happened, but I do know You love me and share my grief. I love You. . .

Acceptance flowed through her. No longer was there just resignation about Neal's death. A love for Jesus Christ was now uppermost in her heart, and Julia knew that the seemingly invincible barrier that had prevented her from knowing the ultimate joy of His presence had been broken down.

Sleep evaded her now. She got up out of bed and walked over to the window. The street lights dotted throughout Central Park were like illuminations of hope in an otherwise dark world. They reminded her of the stained glass windows. Julia smiled, thinking of the light that had shone through them bringing radiance and loveliness to all who would stop and take in their beauty.

Now the inexhaustible beauty of the Lord was with her. She was no longer on the outside looking in, but His pure light had invaded her—His love and comfort were accessible once more.

Julia looked down at her wedding ring. She felt almost ready to take it off. Her fingers grasped it and began to pull it slowly over her knuckle, but she remembered the day Neal had placed it there and she pushed the circlet of gold back again. The telephone rang, jolting her thoughts.

Adam's voice made Julia cry out, "Oh, Adam, I finally have accepted Neal's death! I can't even begin to explain all that I have just experienced, but I do know that I have a peace that I haven't known before!"

"Oh, Julia, I'm so thankful for you. It's what I've prayed for ever since we met."

"Thank you for your prayers, Adam. Oh, I wish you were here, there's so much I want to talk to you about."

"I wish I were, too, Julia."

There was something in his voice that made Julia ask, "Is something wrong, Adam?"

There was a pause and then he said, quietly, "I guess you didn't watch the news this evening?"

"No, Adam. Whatever has happened?" Alarm had crept into her voice.

"There won't be any need to advertise my computer anymore."

"But why?"

"International Computers just announced today that they expect to dominate the market with an economy-priced computer that has all the features mine has. Of course, they are able to manufacture it way below my cost. . . ."

"Oh, Adam, I can hardly believe it. I'm so sorry. But surely there is something you can do."

"Right now I realize I will not be able to compete with their price. They have really undercut me. It will mean the end of my company. I guess that's what hurts the most—all my employees will have to be let go. . . ."

Adam's voice sounded so defeated. How Julia wished she had stayed in San Francisco.

She longed to be able to put her arms around him and comfort this man who had been so caring to her.

"I know this will sound trite, Adam, but God must have a reason for all this..."

"I know He does, Julia. Right now, I feel as if my whole world has caved in. It will take time to pick up the pieces again. But, I know nothing has changed. I am still loved by Him."

"And I love you, too, Adam. Please believe that."

"Oh, Julia, I have longed to hear you say that. But now I have nothing to offer you."

"I only want you, Adam." Julia thought for a moment. "Remember you once said that perhaps God needed more of our time?"

"Yes, I remember, Julia. We were in your car, coming back from Long Island. I remember everything we've ever said to each other. Those words have kept coming back to me tonight. Maybe God wants me to serve Him full-time. I just don't know yet."

"Adam, whatever happens, I know you have so much to offer Him. There's a world that needs your caring..." Julia thought of his tenderness with Alexandra. "How's your newfound aunt, Adam? Have you told her?"

"Yes. She's very much like you, Julia. She said she knew that this must mean a new beginning for me—not the end...."

Julia's heart ached for him. "Oh, Adam, I do so wish I were with you."

"No more than I do, Julia."

"Does Georgina know about this?"

Adam laughed hollowly. "Oh, yes. I had dinner with her tonight, to tell her that there was absolutely no hope of our getting together again. She heard the news about the rival computer on her car radio as she was driving to the restaurant to meet me. Very astutely, she recognized the consequences, realizing that my company would soon be folding. Over dinner she told me that France was beckoning her once more..." Adam laughed again. "At least my computer's demise has helped settle one of my problems!"

There was a conscious feeling of relief that swept through Julia. Georgina was no longer a factor in their lives. She would more than likely marry the Frenchman—leaving no more obstacles in Julia's mind.

"I'm very glad, Adam. I hope she will be happy. But she could never be as happy as I will be with you!"

"Julia...do you mean you want to marry me, even though I will lose my company?"

"I haven't fallen in love with a company, just the incredible man whom God has brought into my life."

There were tears in her eyes as Julia looked down at her wedding ring. "Adam, would you hold on for a few seconds, please?" She put down the telephone and very slowly took off the gold ring and laid it on her Bible.

She picked up the telephone again, and whispered, "Adam, I just took off my wedding ring. I'll cherish it always, but now I accept that it's part of the past...."

Chapter
—15—

The days leading up to Thanksgiving flew by. They were difficult ones for Julia especially when she had walked into the agency, after returning from San Francisco, and had seen all the finished layouts for launching Adam's computer sales compaign. Loving him, the hurt was deep. Yet she knew he had accepted the great disappointment, and was now eager to learn from it just what God wanted him to do with his life.

Patrick and Marianne were amazed by Adam's reaction. "I only hope I would be as accepting if the agency came crashing down around my feet," Patrick had commented.

"I believe you would be," Julia had said, thoughtfully. "Adam has helped me to see so many things in the light of the Lord's plan for each of our lives. Sometimes we have to go through painful experiences before we are sensitive enough to see how much the world needs His love."

Adam called her each night, and he and Julia talked and prayed together—asking God to show them what their future should be.

The Kingsley family tree that Julia had received from the research agency in England had intrigued Adam. "Though completely impoverished, it's nice to know that I belong to a family who once owned the mantlepiece and paneling in your parents' living room! I can always visit my link with the past, Julia. Perhaps one day you and I can pay a call on my old ancestral home in England."

It was ironic that Julia had traced Adam's heritage and that it should turn out that there was no inheritance. Yet, she had always wanted to escape her own roots. Marrying Adam would mean beginning all over again.

● ● ●

Julia packed her suitcase for the trip to her family home—discarding several dressy outfits at the last moment for more casual clothes. No one ever quite knew what Lorraine Taylor would organize on the spur of the moment, but Julia remembered that in her old room she had left several dresses hanging in the closet, that would be suitable in an emergency.

For the drive to her parents' home, she decided to wear an outfit she had bought at I. Magnin's in San Francisco. She had seen it in the window and had made straight for the department where it could be purchased. Her long, lithe figure did justice to the superb tailoring.

The beautifully-cut, charcoal gray gabardine pants, and the soft-tie, pale gray silk blouse looked as if they had been custom made for her. A dusty pink, loose fitting wool jacket with a rolled collar completed the outfit.

Julia looked at herself critically in the mirrow. Her long gold chains were needed as an accent. She had parted her lustrous hair in the middle and had brushed it loosely so that it hung in a shining curve on her shoulders.

Glancing at her watch she saw that the time was almost 10 A.M. If she were to miss the traffic, she would have to leave immediately.

Julia rushed off the elevator in the basement

and walked quickly to her car. As she drove up the ramp and on to Fifth Avenue, she saw that many other people had the same idea that she did—to get out of the city for Thanksgiving.

The drive to Long Island was tedious. Cars were bumper-to-bumper for several miles, until she began to near where her parents lived.

Her mind was so wrapped up in Adam. How she wished she could be spending Thanksgiving with him.

There will be other Thanksgivings together, she thought and a warm feeling swept through her, imagining her life with him. She remembered the previous drive to her parents' home when Adam was by her side. It all seemed so long ago. So much had happened. There was still an ache in her heart for all that Adam had suffered these last few days. They had decided to wait a few weeks before either she would fly back to San Francisco, or Adam would fly east to be with her for a while. Until then she would remember their love for one another...

Julia spent many wonderful Thanksgivings with Neal, but now she knew it was all in the past and she would be forever grateful for the joy she had known with him.

Turning into the drive leading to the family

home, Julia brushed away the tears—not wanting her parents to see any sadness. Today, there was so much to live for. . .

Her mother had heard the car in the driveway and the front door opened wide, welcoming Julia home. She got out of the car and reached in to get the beautiful spray of flowers she had brought for her mother.

"Happy Thanksgiving, Mother! It's so good to be home!"

Lorraine Taylor was a little surprised by the energy of Julia's greeting, but she was nevertheless overjoyed with it and the flowers.

Carrying them into the house, she called over her shoulder, "We'll get the luggage later, Julia. I have a gift for you, too."

Julia was met in the hall by her father, who gave her an enormous bearlike hug. "Welcome home, dear Julia, I've missed seeing you."

Julia could not speak—a feeling of love and appreciation for him and her mother flooded through her. Her father took her hand and began to lead her toward the living room.

"Come, meet some guests. . ."

Julia's heart sank. She had noticed a car that did not belong to her family in the driveway, and had hoped that it did not mean that her ever-scheming mother was on another matchmaking mission. Julia had expected a quiet Thanksgiving with her parents. Graciously, she managed a smile by saying "swiss cheese" to herself as she entered the living room.

Julia stopped—rooted to the spot.

She couldn't believe her eyes!

Standing by the fireplace was Adam, his arms outstretched to her. Alexandra was sitting in an armchair close by.

"Adam!" Julia ran over to him, and for the next few moments was oblivious of anyone or anything except exhilarating, overwhelming joy of being in his arms.

They kissed, and she looked up into his eyes, still unable to believe he was really there. The others in the room looked on with great pleasure at Julia's response to seeing Adam.

"You didn't tell me you were coming!" Then she said, with mock severity, "Is that why you called me so early last night? You said you had an engagement you had to go to . . ." The words tumbled out of Julia and her parents and Alexandra laughed to see her bewilderment and joy.

"Yes, I had an engagement to get to the airport with Alexandra and fly here to be with you for Thanksgiving!" His eyes sparkled with laughter and love, watching the usually composed Julia completely at a loss.

"There must have been a great deal of 'covert' phone calls between you and my parents," Julia added, still trying to comprehend all the planning that had gone on behind her back.

Her mother smiled and said, "There certainly were, Julia. But, don't judge me—you have been a little 'covert' yourself. You didn't even tell me about you and Adam . . . I had to find out about your romance from Alexandra."

"I had planned to tell you today, over Thanksgiving dinner," Julia said, apologetically.

She went over to Alexandra and kissed her, but still held on to Adam's hand. "I'm so glad you were well enough to come for a visit."

"Oh, it's more than a visit," Lorraine Taylor insisted. "Alexandra is going to live with us for as long as she likes. New York is where all her old friends are. She's going to be kept busy for quite some time with all the reunions—*and* helping me with all my charity work."

"That's right, Julia," Alexandra said, a grateful smile on her face. "I'm also going to be kept very busy with the project in . . ."

Lorraine Taylor interrupted her quickly, "Not now, Alexandra!"

Julia looked at both of them, realizing her mother had another surprise up her sleeve.

Adam interjected, "Alexandra's moving here means we can use the condo as our home, until we decide what the future holds for us."

Julia's face lit up. "I could work at the agency out there—at least for a while. And I can keep an eye on Rebecca, who apparently is doing so well. Bob Coleman called me yesterday and said he didn't know how the agency managed without her!"

"That is really great, Julia," Adam said, hugging her to him again.

Julia's father said, "You know, there's another reason for Adam being here, Julia. I wanted to talk to him about two projects that I had in mind. Firstly, I asked him if he would consider joining my company—I could really use his expertise. But he turned me down, saying, very graciously, that he felt God wanted him to work in a full-time ministry somewhere."

Adam exchanged smiles with James Taylor, who went on to say, "That led perfectly into the other project I had in mind. For some time several of my Christian friends on Wall Street have wanted to use some of their foundation money for starting rehabilitation centers to reach some of the young people so caught up in drugs. Not just in this country, but around the world. I asked Adam if he would be willing to head up an organization that would be used to establish homes for these young drug addicts."

Adam took Julia's hands and kissed them. "As I listened to your father I was conscious that this was the answer to our prayers, Julia. I believe that God wants you and I to help take care of the Rebeccas of this world, establishing homes where young people like her can begin again. Would you be willing to help me?"

Julia smiled, tearfully. "Oh, yes, Adam. . . I believe too that this is the answer to our prayers." The pieces of her life were beginning to fit together and the joy in Adam's face made her feel as if her heart could not quite contain all that was happening.

Lorraine Taylor said, excitedly, "Alexandra is going to help me form a committee for the rehabilitation homes, Julia. Now, that's *one* committee I *do* expect you to serve on," she said, with a hint of reproach.

"You can count on me, Mother." Julia looked at her mother, and they both sensed that a deeper relationship was developing between them.

Alexandra questioned, "But how will Julia

be able to find time if she's busy with . . . ?"

Lorraine Taylor hurried over to Alexandra and helped her out of the armchair. "We're not discussing that at the moment, dear Alexandra." Julia's mother wagged a reprimanding finger at her. "Come, I want your advice, Alexandra, about the flowers I arranged for the centerpiece in the dining room." She started walking with her toward the door. "They don't seem to look quite right . . ."

Julia laughed at her mother's obvious scheming. Adam winked at Julia as Lorraine Taylor summed her husband to help also.

"My dear, I've never helped you with the flowers before—*ever*!" he protested as she led him and Alexandra out of the living room. He turned and smiled at Julia and Adam before he closed the doors.

For a few seconds, Julia and Adam just stood and looked at each other. The love in their eyes seemed to spill over and fill the room.

Julia walked over to Adam and they kissed. The whole world was far removed. They were only conscious of the intensity of their love.

She lay her head on Adam's chest, her eyes closed—wanting only to feel his arms around her. She felt so safe. She had finally found and accepted all the love that had been waiting for her.

Her love for Adam knew no bounds now. Gone were any fears or guilt about Neal.

Adam took her hand and looked down at the third finger of her left hand, now bare of Neal's wedding ring. Adam looked at Julia, understanding all she must have felt when she had removed it.

He put his hand into his breast pocket and pulled out an exquisite diamond ring.

"This belonged to my grandmother— Alexandra gave it to me. She wanted you to have it, Julia."

Tears welled up in her eyes as Adam placed it on her finger.

"It's so beautiful," Julia whispered, touching the brilliant antique ring that was part of Adam's heritage.

"Oh, Adam, I still can't really believe all this is happening!"

"You will, darling Julia, you will." He kissed her again, and then said laughingly, "Your mother has even agreed to a small wedding— just the family and a few close friends, like Patrick and Marianne."

Julia laughed with him, still fingering her engagement ring.

Then her mood changed. "What else is going on that I don't know about?"

Adam shrugged his shoulders, an almost innocent look on his face.

"Now I know my mother is up to something else," Julia said wonderingly. "Alexandra almost gave it away. And I noticed *you* knew what it was all about, too!" Julia playfully jabbed her finger in Adam's chest. "Please tell me, I promise I won't let on I know anything," she said, pleadingly, but Adam only shook his head.

"Sorry. You'll have to wait. I don't want to get on the wrong side of your mother!"

He took her in his arms again and silenced her with a long, intense kiss that sent Julia reeling with its fervor.

A gong sounded in the hall, summoning them to Thanksgiving dinner. Julia straightened her hair, still breathless from his kiss.

Adam offered her his arm and together they walked out of the living room to join the others.

"There's so *much* to be thankful for this Thanksgiving, I hardly know where to start," Julia said, her eyes misting over.

"Why don't we start by thanking our Lord for this love we have together in Him?" Adam said, his arm tightly around her shoulder.

"Yes," Julia said appreciatively, "and we'll go on thanking Him through our lifetime. . . ."

Chapter
—16—

That Thanksgiving Day was one Julia would always cherish. When she had walked into the living room and had seen Adam standing there it seemed as if her life were complete once more. Now, brushing her hair before the mirror in her bedroom in New York, she still could not grasp all the happiness that had come into her life. . .

She looked down at her engagement ring. The diamond's brilliance caught the rays of the morning sunlight streaming in her windows. The prisms radiated a rainbow of colors around the room.

Julia smiled, enjoying the welcome intrusion of light. It seemed to symbolize for her all the love and hope she was experiencing.

Today, she was meeting Adam at 11 A.M. He had decided to stay in Manhattan instead of out on Long Island, so that he could both be near Julia and could meet with her father's Christian business friends.

Julia walked over to the window and could see Adam's hotel through the trees in Central Park. She wondered which room was his, whether he was looking out of his window at her apartment house at this very moment. She leaned her head against the window alcove, thinking of how her life had changed...

The snow had melted in the park, leaving small pockets of white dotted here and there. Gone was the illusion of an enchanted principality set amid the towering steel and concrete. skyscrapers of Manhattan. Life seemed to have returned to normal, but for Julia she was on the threshold of a brand new chapter. In three weeks she would become Mrs. Adam Kingsley, and together—after their honeymoon—they would begin to work on the rehabilitation ministry.

She turned to look once more at her bedroom. Soon, the furniture would be gone—

treasures she had collected with Neal would either be sold at auction or given away. Julia would have to go through the heartrending experience of disposing of a home that had been gathered together with a loved one.

Julia walked slowly through the apartment as if she were mentally saying farewell to each item. Letting go of the past was a necessity, if she were to live freely in the future . . .

An unexpected sob wracked Julia. "I'll always love you, Neal," she whispered, haltingly. Only time would be able to give her a completely objective love. The apartment held too many memories. Julia knew she had to act decisively from now on. The next few weeks would be difficult ones.

She turned to look at the hall closet and slowly opened the door. On the floor, lying where she had put them the day they had brought back an agonizing reminder of Neal, were the white skates. His note, found so unexpectedly in one of them, had brought her such sorrow. Deep in thought, Julia picked up the skates and straightened the laces. Today was the time for her to begin to not be afraid of past memories.

Julia reached for her tartan jacket and after putting it on, she slung the skates over her shoulder and opened the front door.

Adam was waiting for her at his hotel...

• • •

Julia pushed her way through the revolving doors of the St. Regis, a smile of anticipation on her face. Adam was standing in the lobby, reading a newspaper. She walked quietly over to him and surprised him with a kiss on his cheek.

"Hi, my handsome fiance. I've missed you so..."

The sight of Julia's radiantly beautiful face smiling up at him made Adam rapidly close the newspaper. Taking her in his arms he kissed her on the lips, whispering, "I thought the time would never come until you were with me once more."

He noticed the white skates. His eyebrows raised in question to Julia.

"Let's go to Rockefeller Plaza," she said, her eyes filled with love for him.

"You're sure you really want to, Julia? It won't be too painful?" His eyes searched hers tenderly.

She shook her head. "I'm learning to not only love again, Adam, but to live again..."

He put his arm around her shoulder and without any more conversation, escorted her out of the hotel on to 58th Street and hailed a taxi.

They sat close together, silently enjoying each other's company. Julia held Adam's hand tightly—as if needing his strength. She watched the traffic, snarled in gigantic tie-ups. The taxi driver rolled down his window to shout at an offending delivery truck that barred their way. It was all part of the city she loved. She looked up at Adam, their eyes meeting in amusement, then changing instantly to one of love.

The taxi pulled up at Rockefeller Center, and they both alighted. While Adam paid the driver, Julia looked up at the 70-story RCA Building that always had the effect of dwarfing her with its immensity; then Adam took her elbow and they began to walk toward the skating rink on the lower level.

His arm went around her waist and Julia felt the exciting closeness of him. Suddenly, Adam stopped. Looking down at her he said, "I can't wait any longer to give you these!"

Adam pulled an envelope out of his coat pocket and handed it to her. Puzzled, she looked at it for a moment and saw it was from a travel agency.

Inside were two airline tickets to England. "For our honeymoon, Julia!" He laughed as he saw her enormous brown eyes light up in amazement.

"The tickets are part of the surprise your family and I have been working on."

Julia's heart turned over, thinking of being in England with Adam. "This is enough of a surprise," she whispered, still looking at the airline tickets.

Adam raised her chin with his hand and kissed her gently. "Kingsley Manor is for sale and your mother and father want to donate the down payment. The rest will be raised by your mother's committee and your father's Wall Street friends. Julia, it could be our home, but more importantly it could be the headquarters for our ministry. From what I'm told, it is perfect for a rehabilitation center. The house has at least fifteen bedrooms and . . ."

Julia put her hand over his lips. "Stop! Please! I can't take it all in. You've really been working behind my back!" Her eyes danced with laughter.

"We didn't want to tell you until we were sure we could buy Kingsley Manor. Do you mind, Julia?" Adam held her at arm's length. "Tell me if you do."

"Mind? How could I mind, Adam? Being with you at Kingsley Manor? Working together for something we both believe in for our Lord?"

They continued their walk toward the skating rink, when Adam stopped, deep in thought. "Do you think we could ever get your parents to return the mantel and paneling to Kingsley Manor?" He suppressed a smile, but his eyes were twinkling.

Julia threw her head back and laughed. "I believe you could talk my mother into anything!"

As they went on walking, they were only conscious of their love and joy in one another...

Tears were sparkling in Julia's eyes. "Oh, how I love you, Adam..."

Gathering her into his arms, Adam held her close to him and whispered, "And I love you, dearest Julia...."

Rhapsody Romances

- ☐ **Another Love**, Joan Winmill Brown   3906
- ☐ **The Candy Shoppe**, Dorothy Abel   3884
- ☐ **The Heart That Lingers**, June Masters Bacher   3981
- ☐ **Love's Tender Voyage**, Joan Winmill Brown   3957
- ☐ **Promise Me Forever**, Colette Collins   3973
- ☐ **The Whisper of Love**, Dorothy Abel   3965
- ☐ **If Love Be Ours**, Joan Winmill Brown   4139
- ☐ **One True Love**, Arlene Cook   4163
- ☐ **Reflection of Love**, Susan Feldhake   4201
- ☐ **Until Then**, Dorothy Abel   4171
- ☐ **Until There Was You**, June Masters Bacher   4198
- ☐ **With All My Heart**, June Masters Bacher   4104
- ☐ **Forever Yours**, Arlene Cook   4383
- ☐ **Let Me Love Again**, Joan Winmill Brown   4392
- ☐ **My Heart To Give**, Carmen Leigh   4368
- ☐ **The Tender Melody**, Dorothy Abel   4287
- ☐ **Touched By Diamonds**, Colette Collins   4279
- ☐ **When Love Shines Through**, June Masters Bacher 4309

$2.95 each

At your local bookstore or use this handy coupon for ordering.

HARVEST HOUSE PUBLISHERS
1075 ARROWSMITH, EUGENE, OREGON 97402

Please send me the book(s) I have checked above. I am enclosing $_____ (please add 50¢ per copy to cover postage and handling). Send check or money order—no cash or C.O.Ds. Please allow four weeks for delivery.

Name _____

Address _____

City _____ State _____ Zip _____

Phone _____

Dear Reader:

We would appreciate hearing from you regarding the Rhapsody Romance series. It will enable us to continue to give you the best in inspirational romance fiction.

Mail to: Rhapsody Romance Editors

Harvest House Publishers, 1075 Arrowsmith, Eugene, OR 97402

1. What most influenced you to purchase **LET ME LOVE AGAIN**?
   - ☐ The Christian Story
   - ☐ Cover
   - ☐ Backcover copy
   - ☐ Recommendations
   - ☐ Other Rhapsody Romances you've read
   - ☐ _____

2. Your overall rating of this book:
   ☐ Excellent ☐ Very good ☐ Good ☐ Fair ☐ Poor

3. Which elements did you find most appealing in this book?
   - ☐ Heroine
   - ☐ Hero
   - ☐ Setting
   - ☐ Story line
   - ☐ Love Scenes
   - ☐ Christian message

4. How many Rhapsody Romances have you read all together?
   (Choose one) ☐ 1-2 ☐ 3-6 ☐ 7-10 ☐ Over 11

5. How likely would you be to purchase other Rhapsody Romances?
   - ☐ Very likely
   - ☐ Somewhat likely
   - ☐ Not very likely
   - ☐ Not at all

6. Please check the box next to your age group.
   - ☐ Under 18
   - ☐ 18-24
   - ☐ 25-34
   - ☐ 35-39
   - ☐ 50-54
   - ☐ Over 55

Name _____

Address _____

City _____ State _____ Zip _____